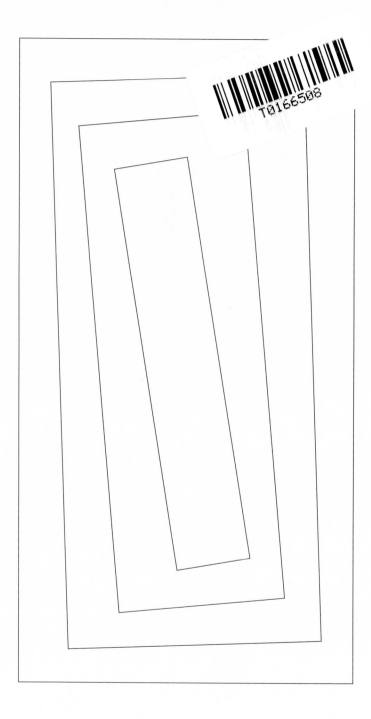

# THE AGENTS

## GRÉGOIRE COURTOIS

### TRANSLATED BY
## RHONDA MULLINS

COACH HOUSE BOOKS, TORONTO

First English-language edition. Originally published as *Les Agents* by Le
Quartanier, 2019.

Liberté • Égalité • Fraternité
RÉPUBLIQUE FRANÇAISE
AMBASSADE DE FRANCE AU CANADA

*The Agents* is published in partnership with the
Toronto Cultural Service of the French
Embassy in Canada.

LIBRARY AND ARCHIVES CANADA CATALOGUING IN PUBLICATION

Title: The agents / Grégoire Courtois ; translated by Rhonda Mullins.
Other titles: Agents. English
Names: Courtois, Grégoire, author. | Mullins, Rhonda, translator.
Description: Translation of: Les agents.
Identifiers: Canadiana (print) 20210300043 | Canadiana (ebook)
20210300051 | ISBN 9781552454329 (softcover) | ISBN 9781770566880
(EPUB) | ISBN 9781770566897 (PDF)
Subjects: LCGFT: Novels.
Classification: LCC PQ2703.O97 A6413 2022 | DDC 843/.92—dc23

*The Agents* is available as an ebook: ISBN 978 1 77056 688 0 (EPUB), ISBN 978
1 77056 689 7 (PDF)

Purchase of the print version of this book entitles you to a free digital copy.
To claim your ebook of this title, please email sales@chbooks.com with proof
of purchase. (Coach House Books reserves the right to terminate the free
digital download offer at any time.)

# TABLE OF CONTENTS

There is no such thing as the end of the world.

What we call the end of the world is a cat running and turning the corner in a corridor. It's the shadow of the shadow of a shadow, the shape of which seems familiar but in reality has no more substance than the wind that will scatter our ashes.

The end of the world is an idea, a concept, and the concept sinks its black roots into every one of us, drawing from us, our entire lives, the sweet sap of our personal, final, inescapable, and instantaneous destruction.

There are as many ends of the world as there are worlds, and each one takes shape for each person based on their habitat, that particular narrow, empty universe they occupy and cross through.

But the end of the world, the only true end of the world, which would be obvious to all of us, is somewhere far away, in a barren land where no one will ever set foot.

It is our lot to live in worlds that exist only for us. It is our lot to suffer apocalypses of which we alone understand the symbols and the searing revelation, which remain sadly hermetic to our brethren, who are terrorized by images of their own destruction.

And yet our feet kick up dust, and our flesh touches flesh and feels the sweat that drips from it, the blood we draw from it, and we slide along clammy skin and kilometres of worn carpet and foolishly staid existences, which are, for each of us, stubbornly and until rapture, the same.

It all seems so real. And we seem so real, so alive, so aware that the days that are behind us cannot be the ones that will follow.

It is the ultimate question that we ask ourselves without asking it and whisper to ourselves without hearing it.

But even if it is not the case – if it is not the end of the world, the true end of the world, what we are witnessing, what did the agents who came before us also witness, and others still before them, for so long that no one knows when it started,

if it is not the true, exact end of all things, which removes from humans their humanity and from objects their reason to remain rather than turn to dust,

if it is not the end of the world, of the days of despair we are living, disguised as joy at being here rather than nowhere –

if it is not the end of the world, then what is it?

# I.
# STATUS

AGENT IDENTIFICATION:
SOUTH QUARTER \ TOWER 35S \ 122ND FLOOR \
SECTOR Y1 \ CUBICLE 314 \
FEED: LOCAL NEWS \ 08:04

PERSONALIZED NEWS
The sun has been up for 37 minutes and 12 seconds. If it were not overcast, the sun would be streaming into your cubicle in 23 minutes and 57 seconds.

You are Agent Élisabeth. This morning, you are in a good mood.

You got up early, and your horoscope shows that the alignment of the stars will foster unanticipated on-the-job performance.

It's a day of purpose, a day to be bold, and the agents in your sector will have many opportunities to increase their productivity.

Armed with solid ambition and nerves of steel, you can achieve significant progress in the near term, provided you put the odds in your favour by keeping your eyes glued to your work.

Certain people around you, located in sectors Y2 and S1 (cubicles 305 to 311, and cubicles 234 to 240), will be a bad influence and, with their tendency toward idleness, could put your professional activity in jeopardy. It is up to you to avoid them so that your name is not associated with theirs when they reach the final social stage tolerated and the company initiates disciplinary measures against them.

GENERAL NEWS
The bathrooms on your floor (122) are closed for high-pressure cleaning. They will reopen at 11:15.

Please wait in your cubicle until then and start working to avoid employees gathering in sector M2.

There is sufficient natural light, so we recommend you not use secondary light sources, to conserve energy. Thank you for following these instructions, which are in everyone's interest.

# 1.
# THE OFFICE

The place where we live is the place where we work. We are agents.

It is our status, our identity, our source of pride.

We do our work in front of machines from another century that purr like pets, while behind the tinted windows of our office, thick cloud cover creeps east to west.

We are armed.

Time and experience have provided us the gunpowder and the shot. We have a stockpile, and we use it when we need it.

Against others, against ourselves, against time as it stands still, we wage the eternal battle of something against nothing and, when one of our enemies drops dead to the ground, we are delighted that chance has chosen us to carry the flame of activity for a few more days.

Without combat, we might not know that our presence here is necessary. That's why we are always fighting.

We have five breaks a day, and we have the night.

These moments are the temporal battlefields of our war.

From 05:00 to 08:00, we work.

From 08:15 to 11:15, we work.

From 11:30 to 14:30, we work again.

From 14:45 to 17:45, we work some more.

From 18:45 to 21:00, we keep working.

And from 21:15 to 00:15, we work.

Outside of these times, we are free, and we fight to try to stay that way.

The office is our life.

No one can remember a time when humans lived outside their workplace, or distant centuries when work was just an activity like any other.

What we know is that lifeless days now stretch out before us without anything to do other than boil water, drink it, kill, and avoid being killed.

This world is what our predecessors left us; they too had inherited it.

These cubicles are our homes, this carpet our earth, these colleagues our fellow citizens, and woe betide any who renounce these fundamental principles, because for them, there is only the street, far below. Even though none of us have ever set foot there, even though we cannot make it out through the floor-to-ceiling windows, we know that, as harsh as it is for us, as difficult as our existence is, there is nothing worse than the street.

# 2.
## THE GUILD

We do not walk alone through the heavy sadness of our days.

We are part of a group, a band of brothers and sisters – a guild.

We have our tensions, differences, and rifts, but we diligently follow the unspoken laws of the group, which is what guarantees our survival.

Some agents walk alone, but that comes with the dark price of constant worry and vigilance, under the threat of assault by a guild that has set its sights on them. These solitary agents are called the Underlins. They are invisible; they hit hard and fast. They work on the 122nd floor, like fearful scavengers, condemned to hide even their shadows in the shadow of the armoured walls. They live a life of fear, alertness, and flight, the door to their cubicles always closed, with no sound escaping that would betray their clandestine activities.

There are the Underlins, and there are the guilds. Because waiting alone for death to come is a job in addition to the one we already have, and waiting for it together gives you a chance to sleep sometimes, while someone keeps watch.

In our guild, there is Solveig, whose body is entirely hairless, because she finds hair vulgar.

The hair on her head, of course, the down on her arms, along with her eyebrows, eyelashes, and anything else that could grow on her, is meticulously removed, so meticulously that her silhouette is the only visual texture she can stand to see sticking out above the surface of the earth.

Solveig believes that the future of agents lies in purity. Purity of mind, of course, but the immaterial can achieve fruition only with the aid and the discipline of the body. Her appearance and her diet, which many reduce to anorexia, reveal a fanatical asceticism, the only path, she tells us, to elevating our condition.

In our guild, there is also Théodore, who once severed all ten of his toes because of a date entered on a calendar known only to him. At the dawn of a new personal era, he thought his toes were good for nothing more than grasping objects like a primate, which he never did, of course. And so, one calm night, with no sound emerging from his cubicle, he amputated what he called 'vestiges of the archaic interface.' Not a cry, not a word, he beat a bloody path toward the future of our species.

Some say he keeps his severed toes in a jar of formaldehyde hidden in his office, but no one has ever dared check or even ask him if the story is true.

Since that time, Théodore has walked faster than other agents along the narrow corridors of the floor, and we have come to understand that speed is what maintains his balance. Go fast or fall: we could have made it our motto and amputated our own toes, but we preferred to abstain, no doubt because Théodore is the only one with the mysterious calendar.

In our guild, there is Laszlo, and even though he doesn't call himself an artist, it is the title we have quite naturally given him. Since his arrival in the office, his entire life seems to have been a long, powerful performance with a changing audience, where every moment can be studied for its purity or complexity, like one of the important components of a surrogate life through art. Laszlo's life is performance, spectacle, or novel. Snippets of his work are disseminated on the public networks with such regularity that some Veep Watchers believe he is not a true agent but rather a Veep producing fiction in a well-appointed studio somewhere far away. Only we know the truth, and we have also calculated how dangerous it may be to keep company with Laszlo, as we risk becoming part of his work, presented to an audience in a distant future, a near future, or an unanticipated present. Information is critical in the office. Revealing anything about our movements or habits on public networks could be fatal. And yet Laszlo remains one of us. Maybe being around him, and then making him part of our guild, was in the end motivated by a secret hope to feel the sudden warmth of exposure, the spotlight of glory, or simply the reassuring tranquility of a useful existence, despite the risks. Laszlo is one of our tickets to the light. If we were to become only minor characters, even formless extras, in his personal novel, at least we will not have been decisively nothing.

In our guild, there is also Clara. Clara used to be a close friend of Laszlo's, but his destructive approach to art drove a wedge between them, so that today their relationship boils down to exchanges of abrupt looks and an infinitesimal number of polite greetings that emerge only a little louder than silence when chance, with its mischievous ways, brings them together.

Clara considers it essential for art and the world to methodically destroy her physical appearance, and this periodic laceration takes different forms, finding its true expression in scarification under anaesthetic, a practice that allows her to alter her appearance flawlessly and cleanly, but that also delivers plenty of intoxicating sensations, such as the numbing of her limbs and the cruel post-operative shock.

According to many documents and photos, Clara used to be an agent with a pleasing face and strong muscles, which is to say a preferred physique, suited to office life, where charisma is respected and agility feared.

Many argue that it is the guilt of having been spoiled by the random gifts of her conception that drove her to such destructive extremes.

Some prefer to suggest that she falsified her documents, gathered from public data, that there is nothing artistic about her current appearance, but that it is the result of a poorly treated congenital deformity.

Yet if any of them had attended Clara's glorious scarlet happening in the office bathroom last season, the unfortunate witnesses never would have doubted the truth nor the extent of her self-mutilation.

# 3.
## CLARA'S SCARLET HAPPENING

It was a morning like any other. Which is to say it held as many unfortunate surprises and disappointments as any other, as many hopes crushed, and as many drab confirmations that our existences keep plunging toward the abyss.

Their individual lights went on one by one starting at 04:30, setting the example for the brightness expected of the day and bringing to life the basement's antique generator, which had been spared by the low nighttime electrical activity. On its meter, numbers started streaming faster again, numbers that everyone had forgotten the significance of as the agents' hot plates came to life to boil water for breakfast.

No one had seen Clara that morning, because people rarely bother with those who are discreet, and particularly because, being part of our guild, she was not authorized to try anything without the protocol of armed engagement. If we had to reduce a wayward Copier to a pulp or initiate hostilities against a troublesome guild, the information was made public on the intranet to give our target time to make a run for it if their courage to face the street was greater than their courage to fight us.

So, that morning, there was no announcement of a public skirmish, and we were going about our activities, indifferent to our neighbours.

No one noticed Clara, who, at 11:16, slowly exited her armoured cubicle, slowly walked down the deserted corridors of the office, and slowly closed the bathroom door behind her, taking the time to lock it.

The air conditioning hummed for a handful of minutes, spreading through the empty corridors millions of dust particles, some of which were probably all that remained of the southern cities that our daily inaction had helped destroy.

For a handful of minutes, numbers accumulated on our computer screens, and we religiously watched them go by like the digital exegetes of the long hermetic apocalypse we were living through.

When nothing was planned during a break, we would generally fill it by continuing our work.

That is when the residents of cubicles in sectors K and L, which is to say near the bathrooms, heard Solveig's voice whisper a repeated call. Théodore lifted above the partition wall a piece of mirror he used to observe the bathroom comings and goings without having to show himself.

He spotted in the reflection Solveig's thin silhouette, recognizable in her white jumpsuit. She was leaning toward the door. He took the risk of peeking into the corridor. He was the only one who did, because he was the only one who knew it wasn't a trap. With one hand, he typed out an instant message to Laszlo:

[chan#M256] THÉODORE: Bathroom – now.
[chan#M256] LASZLO: Why?
[chan#M256] THÉODORE: Solveig XO.

Théodore didn't wait for a response.

XO was our internal emergency code, and it wasn't used lightly. So, Laszlo went, hunched and silent, moving through the corridors with carpets we imagined had been blue but that the feet of agents had made greyish and threadbare.

When he reached the bathroom door, at 11:27, we were already all there, lips vibrating in the cracks to make sounds we hoped would reach Clara.

'Is it a performance?' Théodore asked.

'It's beautiful,' said Laszlo, before the beep of his portable recorder was heard. His show was starting.

'We are in the belly of one of the dark times, contorted amidst the empty, dry entrails of a new insipid day, searching like animals for a sign in the sky that will change our inertia into action, and our action into saga. Whispering to a closed door is what we have found to distinguish today from yesterday, and to ensure the stinking offspring of the past that we deny are stillborn before they can in turn give birth to a more sinister reality. There may be nothing behind the door, no friend or foe, but it's a better life we are calling for. We do not want to go to bed tonight pale and ashamed of having done exactly what we are asked to do every day. Clara was the first – '

'Shut up, Laszlo,' Solveig said, interrupting him. 'I don't want to be in your goddamn novel.'

'We have to break down the door,' Théodore said.

'You break down the door, and your hope that something important is going on behind it will be shattered into pieces,' said Laszlo, whom everyone was ignoring.

'Step aside,' Théodore said. 'Solveig, help me.'

They took a run at it while Laszlo kept watch. Damaging company property was not the sort of thing that went unpunished, and we knew it. The door didn't belong to us. It belonged to everyone, and violating its integrity was an act of aggression toward the guilds and the agents on our floor. Those on floors below and above couldn't care less, of course, because they had their own bathrooms.

So, it was with full knowledge that Théodore and Solveig flung themselves with all their might at the grey plastic and shattered the flimsy lock on the women's bathroom.

'Magnificent,' Laszlo said, when he in turn stepped into the bathroom. 'I don't approve, but it's magnificent.'

We were dumbfounded for long seconds as we took in the scene, while the subtle odour of stale smoke hung in the air. War had just broken out deep down inside us. On one side, wearing helmets and inky-black bulletproof suits, was an army of shadowy soldiers flying the dark flag of fascination with beauty. These soulless warriors showed no mercy, no sentiment, and the only things that counted for them were regular manifestations of a universe shaken by the mystical vibration of meaning and form and their fulfilment here on earth. Men and women could die, tear each other apart, their limbs ripped off and cast to the whims of the radioactive winds; these victims weren't important, and no eulogy would honour their memory, because their loss occurred in the interest of the weak passion that still inhabited us a little. This army had simmered in our hearts since our arrival, each one of us, in these anonymous offices, and its furious march kept us upright, forced us to see clearly and not waver in the face of the horror of our thoughts. As terrible as it was, our desire for death was beautiful, and it was all that counted, so that we could keep saying for a while longer that we were human and not animals.

On the other side, faced with this dark army, soldiers offered up their pale flanks to the bayonet. Smeared with soot and blood, ashes and dust, they waged a critical battle in the sticky recesses of our cerebella, a campaign for survival, to ensure our species is not wiped out. For these combatants, nothing meant more than protecting the tissue that prevented our flesh from spilling onto the greyish carpet of the office. It was the instinctive army, blind to the runes, deaf to the drums, that, until its last breath, would fight so that humans beget humans, at the price of all the ugliness.

As a result, we were paralyzed, caught between the desire to save Clara, who was losing her blood before our very eyes, and the fear of interrupting one of the most beautiful works of art that the monotony of the world offered us.

To achieve this perfection, our friend must have spent days, maybe months, doing short blood draws in secret, storing in a refrigerated place pouches of her blood that her obedient body had quickly replaced. Judging from the scarlet expanse of blood coagulating at our feet, her preparations had given her a spectacular amount of hemoglobin. At 11:16 this morning, while we were all still half asleep and wondering what catastrophe would break up the calm of the day, she must have transported her red cargo from her cubicle to the bathroom, flaccid pouches hidden under a shirt looser than normal, a viscous offering to the beauty of the day. Then she barricaded the door from the inside, put her liquid treasure in place, and started the business of gushing mutilation.

The black slit at the crease of her left arm had to be the result of a knife or a scalpel that had severed her brachial artery. Spasmodic spurting onto her forearm created a river of blood that ran into her open palm and dripped from each finger into the tranquil pool where she was lying, while, planted in her other arm, a needle connected to a plastic pouch was feeding her as much vital fluid as she was losing.

Clara had imagined this process, spent weeks collecting the blood needed to pull it off, and had no doubt calculated the exact duration of the performance, the point of no return when the pouches of blood would no longer be enough to replace the precious pints she was spilling onto the white tile.

Finally, there was the toilet paper. Long, carefully wadded clumps were placed on the floor to contain the pool of blood. If we could have hovered three metres above the scene, the tableau would have been sublime: Clara sitting against the drab wall, her legs bathing in a scarlet expanse, the contours of which formed a star with unequal spikes on the tiled surface.

In addition to forming this pattern, the toilet paper had a function: it indicated to us that what we were witnessing was in no way a depressive act reached at the end of her painful journey. This subtle drawing confirmed to us that, on the contrary, it had been staged, that this event was intentional, that it had been planned and thought through to become part of the annals of art history and not the sad history of neurosis.

Clara had done her happening for art, for beauty, and if the operation had killed her, if we hadn't found her in time and she had perished, bled out on the reddened tile of the bathroom, she would have succeeded in what everyone, in one way or another, was trying to do: to lend our dreary and confined existence an end that was sufficiently dignified, because the rest of it never had been.

# 4.
# THE REPLACEMENTS

Mid-month is the best time for attacks against guilds.

It's the red period, when every act, every movement, must be considered, useful, and necessary, when the slightest move could end in a mortal clash. During this critical period, just one of these clashes could result in the total annihilation of a guild.

When you belong to a guild, dying mid-month means dying twice. A first time truly, disappearing from your cubicle forever, being thrown to the street, or dying for good, which amounts to the same thing; and then a second time, because your place is given to someone else, someone younger, called a replacement, straight out of the institute, and who at the end of the month will receive only half a salary, often not enough to survive.

The mid-month replacement, with their first half salary, is a half replacement. They are half alive and, as a result, already half dead.

Not knowing the rules of the office they are joining, not knowing the names and faces to avoid, mid-month replacements have to be nice, intelligent, and tactical to hope to keep their cubicle another month and earn enough money to stay. Mid-month replacements normally last a little less than a week before being eliminated. If they are cunning, they can hold out up to ten days before succumbing, but in 99 per cent of cases, mid-month replacements don't live long enough to see the next month and simply disappear, fleeting glimmers of innocent rejuvenation in the infinite night of our world.

Generally speaking, mid-month or not, a replacement is already prey, as frail as a bird fallen from the nest, with no way to feed themselves or weapons to defend themselves, skinny and condemned to become even more so if no agent takes them under their wing.

It is custom that guilds that have just lost a member take the newly arrived replacement under their wing, training them and protecting them as much as possible. In such cases, the effort must pay off, so that the young agent joins the guild and defends the collective interest.

Few guilds train mid-month replacements. They prefer to grow stronger or prepare a rapid response, rather than wasting time and money maintaining a neophyte who can't even buy a drop of water.

Successful mid-month attacks handicap a guild for at least two weeks. A mid-month attack leading to the loss of a member of the targeted guild is often just a prelude to a bid for complete destruction of the guild in question, assault after assault, its members obliterated one by one, their bodies decomposed by acid clouds, sent back to the darkness of a world that is even less of a choice than this one. If the targeted guild is destroyed before the end of the month, the attacking guild takes over training replacements who arrive during this period, expanding its cubicle holdings and in turn its territorial supremacy.

They say that higher up in the tower, guilds have managed to seize entire floors of offices, and that, even higher still, all-out wars pit hundreds of men and women against each other in deadly fights waged in cold no-man's-lands. These floors with no cubicles are supposedly used only as battlefields for enormous guilds with all-powerful generals.

Other, even more incredible stories make the rounds about these large-scale battles. Some agents claim that elsewhere in the city merciless wars are rampant, pitting company against company, tower against tower, agent against agent. But no one really believes these stories, because no one here knows how to get to other floors of the tower, and the possibility of leaving the tower itself – in other words, going through the street – is the stuff of legend, stories told to replacements as fodder for dreams, so they do not immediately founder in the nightmarish reality of our condition, which is that we are stuck here, from the moment we pass through the 8-Char Door to the moment we die.

They need to keep that hope for a little while, so that they understand in their own time and are not too angry with us for having brought them into the world, regardless of whether we are their parents.

Hope is what keeps us going in the early days, when the walls of the cubicle seem to be closing in, our space so confined. And it takes a little while to give up hope, prisoners as we are of animal instincts that whisper in our ear that this life has meaning.

Every time we see a replacement arrive, even though we know that most of them will soon be annihilated, we look at them with understanding and envy, beings full of the hope that has abandoned us, leaving not even its breath.

Because we were all once replacements. At the beginning of our career, we all fought the entire office before gaining enough value to join a guild or melt into the anonymous payroll.

We crawled in the shadows along this imposed, dangerous path, our only comfort the mad idea that things would work out, that life couldn't be just this, a perpetual fight that gives us only the right to crawl a little while longer.

And we envy that irrational hope. Despite the risks, and the high mortality rate, we secretly want to be a replacement again, naive, a carefree newcomer, who nurses within them a plant they do not realize will never flower.

We don't talk about it, but we often think about it, particularly when the general news feed announces the arrival of a replacement, and, through the crack of our doors, we see them wander the corridors searching for their cubicle, scanning their new environment like an animal being stalked, knocking timidly at doors to ask for advice and being immediately thrown onto the street by the company for speaking to the wrong person. Often, we think they could have been us, that we could have been them, and that the endless luck we enjoyed might not have been enough, that one moment of inattention, one second of letting down our guard, could have cost us our cubicle and the safety it represents.

What becomes of young newcomers fired in the first few days? All we know is they disappear from our floor. If their life comes to a neat end and their consciousness finds eternal rest in the clammy limbs of eternity, we often regret not having met this soothing fate sooner.

We too would be dead, calm and serene, far from the office and the constant vigilance it requires. Everything would be simpler, and the ordeal would be over.

Or maybe not – no one really knows what happens to employees who are fired.

And if they don't die, and they are thrown onto the street, in our suffering we still think ourselves lucky to have avoided the pitfalls and assaults of the early days. Unlucky to be alive, but lucky to be alive here rather than elsewhere.

Because elsewhere can only be worse. It is an axiom we learned and that remains rooted in us to save us from errors in judgment.

Rather than walking these aisles, having shelter when it is cold and shade when it is hot, we would be on the street, whatever that means.

We would have no job, no name, no occupation, no goal, abandoned to destiny, poverty, and the worst shame of all, the shame of no longer being an agent.

\#

Milton Banks, actor emeritus from Akzion Studios, was spotted Saturday in the company of Cily Vinière, the young heiress from the west zone of Chicago 3.

According to witnesses, the two stars' physical proximity and mannerisms leave no doubt as to the nature of their relationship (see videos).

Should this romance be officially confirmed, the lovers would become the 16th couple of the year to aspire to the prestigious Rich & Ultra-Rich Award, which in January recognizes the most financially powerful couple in the Confederation.

\#

Josh McGuilick, the failed captain of the Bombay West Flames, defeated in Thursday's finals of the SlashMetal NLE Intercompany Cup, has announced he will be leaving the Chinese-Indonesian team.

During the ninth decan break of this final, spectators noted the toxic atmosphere on the Flames' sidelines when McGuilick deliberately opened fire on his coach, Roy Malalan, with his game weapon. During the post-game press conference, the captain explained that he did it to 'regain control of this team of pussies led by a complete jackass.' A risky tactical choice was seemingly behind McGuilick's anger; he said he 'had no choice but to shut the idiot up.'

Taking advantage of Malalan's extended unconsciousness, treated by the NLE medical team, McGuilick led his team during the entire last decan. Despite racking up points, McGuilick's efforts on the field and the bench weren't enough, and his team was defeated 42 to 31.

Josh McGuilick has not indicated which other clubs he has been in discussions with.

The 17-year-old player from the grey zone of the Indonesian archipelago currently holds the world record in L&C points, all categories and seasons combined, with 36 L(ethal) cards and 79 C(oma) cards.

# 5.
# WORK

The stories live with us, in our midst, like other agents, domesticated creatures whose presence reassures us without their absence worrying us. We know deep down that they are there, somewhere, and that they will end up reappearing, sooner or later.

Stories, anecdotes, and legends are the last refuge for our hope, if any hope remains.

They are the oxygen and the water that remove any doubt that we are alive.

Being dead means no longer hearing stories and no longer telling any.

Being dead means becoming a story that hurtles toward oblivion, reduced to ashes on the particles of time.

Being dead means only working, without anything else around to stop us from realizing that we serve no purpose.

The story of work is the first story an agent learns upon becoming an agent.

It is the first story, the one that teaches them who they are, and why they are here.

In this story that goes back as far as work itself, it is said that there was never a time when work was not the sole reason to be alive.

Work, and the fight to keep it.

Fresh from the institute, incredulous survivors in the second month of our adult existence, we started to ask colleagues questions, always getting the same answers and hearing the same story, so that in turn, later on, we repeated it to the replacements who asked us questions.

We have to work, because our work is our dignity, the only thing that sets us apart from the savages the street swallowed up, whose lives aren't of use even to themselves, impassive electrons launched into the chaotic orbit of their own weakness.

Work is a faith, the ultimate proof that we are human, and it answers the only question that we could ask ourselves: why?

Work is that answer, and that answer holds within it the swollen seed of all the rest: if we stop working, what will there be left for us to do?

As soon as the first rays of sun change the dark, cloudy layer into a cottony mass streaked with dark rain, we station ourselves in front of our screens to follow the evolution of the unimaginable network of machines that manage our world. Set out in eighty lines, one hundred and six columns, and thirty-two levels of sharpness, the batches of information scroll by at a variable pace, depending on importance and urgency. Our eyes scan the raw data that the instructors taught us to decipher at the dawn of our life, in four directions: from top to bottom, from bottom to top, from left to right and right to left, according to a grid that everyone personalizes based on their mood.

We monitor the flow of capital.

We monitor the price of stocks.

We monitor the value of the indexes, the operating reports, the quarterly reports, the mergers and acquisitions, the crashes, the upturns, the births, and the deaths. A fluid maze of numbers and words passes before our eyes like vibrant nature in perpetual bloom.

We all play a role, the same one, and that role guarantees the world runs smoothly.

Agents monitor, and monitoring guarantees their status as agent.

In our first days of work, if we are lucky enough to meet a colleague friendly enough to answer us, we inevitably ask what to do in the event of a problem. What to do if a bug is detected, if a system derails, or if a mistake is made?

The friendly colleague then answers our question with what all agents know:

There is never a mistake in the system.

We don't work to monitor. We monitor to work.

Without work, we would be ugly and savage, useless and unworthy.

That is what the first story tells us, and every day confirms it is true.

# 6.
# THE VEEPS

[chan#sq8837] SOLVEIG: Do you think Cily Vinière will win the award?

[chan#sq8837] LASZLO: What's up with you? Are you becoming a Veep Watcher?

[chan#sq8837] SOLVEIG: I'm just trying to make conversation.

[chan#sq8837] LASZLO: I know.

[chan#sq8837] LASZLO: That's exactly what the general news is for.

[chan#sq8837] LASZLO: To get us talking.

[chan#sq8837] LASZLO: Meanwhile, we forget what's important.

[chan#sq8837] SOLVEIG: Like what?

[chan#sq8837] LASZLO: Like tiny traces of gold in the block of quartz.

[chan#sq8837] LASZLO: It's gold, it shines, it's precious, but if you don't take the time to look properly, you can't see the glittering nuggets. News is made for that, to distract our eyes from the block of quartz and prevent us from seeing the nuggets under our noses.

[chan#sq8837] SOLVEIG: I don't think I give a shit about the nuggets.

[chan#sq8837] LASZLO: You don't want a better life?

[chan#sq8837] LASZLO: A more important job?

[chan#sq8837] LASZLO: A bigger cubicle?

[chan#sq8837] LASZLO: And a different feeling deep down inside each morning that is not hatred or disgust at being where you are, doing what you do?

[chan#sq8837] LASZLO: Don't you want the road that leads from birth to death to be safe and straight and glorious rather than muddy and difficult and winding?

34

[chan#sq8837] LASZLO: Don't you want to become someone rather than remaining no one?

[chan#sq8837] SOLVEIG: I think I just want it to stop.

[chan#sq8837] LASZLO: Because something else is always worse.

[chan#sq8837] SOLVEIG: Exactly.

[chan#sq8837] SOLVEIG: If the company has taught me anything true, it's that.

[chan#sq8837] SOLVEIG: That it's better to fight to keep what you have than to take the chance to find something worse in the illusions we are presented with.

[chan#sq8837] LASZLO: And yet you read the general news every morning.

[chan#sq8837] SOLVEIG: Yes.

[chan#sq8837] SOLVEIG: To entertain myself.

[chan#sq8837] SOLVEIG: Exactly the reason you mention.

[chan#sq8837] SOLVEIG: To divert my eyes from the block of quartz and, most importantly, out of mercy, to stop seeing it, if only for a few moments.

[chan#sq8837] LASZLO: And you never project yourself into it?

[chan#sq8837] LASZLO: You never want it to be your name instead of Cily Vinière's in the news?

[chan#sq8837] SOLVEIG: Honestly, I don't think Cily Vinière exists.

[chan#sq8837] SOLVEIG: I think it's a character that was invented for people like me but that has no actual substance, except in our imagination.

[chan#sq8837] SOLVEIG: I see what is around us, and it makes me think. And the more I think, the more I believe it isn't possible for men and women to come out of an institute and become replacements in those lofty circles.

[chan#sq8837] SOLVEIG: I think there are no lofty circles, that the world is governed by the same machines as the ones that turn on the generator and the air conditioner,

[chan#sq8837] SOLVEIG: by the same machines that do the work we're paid for, and the same ones still that search for stars through the clouds and tell us in the morning exactly what time the sun will never hit our cubicle.

[chan#SQ8837] SOLVEIG: None of the general news stories we read are true.

[chan#SQ8837] SOLVEIG: Cily Vinière doesn't exist,

[chan#SQ8837] SOLVEIG: neither does Milton Banks,

[chan#SQ8837] SOLVEIG: or Josh McGuilick.

[chan#SQ8837] SOLVEIG: It's all just another instalment that has been given a different, realistic form.

[chan#SQ8837] SOLVEIG: But it's not real.

[chan#SQ8837] SOLVEIG: We are all agents.

[chan#SQ8837] SOLVEIG: All men, all women, live in a cubicle and work hard, to be replaced by other agents when they die.

[chan#SQ8837] SOLVEIG: That's the reality I sincerely believe in.

[chan#SQ8837] SOLVEIG: It's mine. And I sincerely believe it because, if it weren't true, and if someone in this world could lead as fabulous a life as Cily Vinière, if such an injustice were possible, our condition would be even more horrible than it already is.

[chan#SQ8837] LASZLO: I would like to think the way you do, but I can't.

[chan#SQ8837] SOLVEIG: But it's so simple. You just have to tell yourself that it's all fiction.

[chan#SQ8837] SOLVEIG: It shouldn't be hard for you.

[chan#SQ8837] SOLVEIG: Imagine that everything you read is invented by machines to relieve your boredom doing a job that involves watching over an infallible system.

[chan#SQ8837] SOLVEIG: Basically, doing nothing.

[chan#SQ8837] LASZLO: But lots of agents think I'm fiction too.

[chan#SQ8837] LASZLO: That I don't live in this office.

[chan#SQ8837] LASZLO: That the story I'm telling of our existence is a fable.

[chan#SQ8837] LASZLO: Do you think they're right too?

[chan#SQ8837] SOLVEIG: Don't be silly.

[chan#SQ8837] LASZLO: I'm serious.

[chan#SQ8837] LASZLO: If I'm real, why would Cily Vinière be an illusion?

[chan#SQ8837] SOLVEIG: Because I've never seen her.

[chan#SQ8837] LASZLO: And if someone had met her, an agent, in this office, would that change your mind?

[chan#SQ8837] SOLVEIG: Do you know an agent who has met Cily Vinière?

[chan#SQ8837] LASZLO: I don't know if I can tell you.

[chan#SQ8837] SOLVEIG: You're making fun.

[chan#SQ8837] SOLVEIG: It's impossible.

[chan#SQ8837] SOLVEIG: How would a Veep come to the office without anyone noticing?

[chan#SQ8837] SOLVEIG: It's ridiculous.

[chan#SQ8837] LASZLO: You can choose not to believe me.

[chan#SQ8837] LASZLO: But you also know that there is always a chance that a highly improbable thing occurs.

[chan#SQ8837] SOLVEIG: Of course.

[chan#SQ8837] LASZLO: If I tell you everything I know, will you let me come to your cubicle tonight?

[chan#SQ8837] SOLVEIG: To do what?

[chan#SQ8837] LASZLO: To see you.

[chan#SQ8837] LASZLO: To be sure you're not fiction.

[chan#SQ8837] SOLVEIG: Do you really know something about Cily Vinière?

[chan#SQ8837] LASZLO: Let me come over tonight and I'll tell you.

[chan#SQ8837] SOLVEIG: Fine.

# 7.
## AN AGENT NAMED PIOTR

When we discovered him, we didn't know how he had arrived in the office and, for a long time after, we barely asked ourselves the question.

Had he arrived like all of us, directly from the institute at the end of a calm month, or had he already lived a thousand lives and roamed different floors and visited different towers before appearing to us?

We didn't know. Maybe he had always been there, absorbed in his duties, a recluse in a single cubicle, from the time when there was only one cubicle, and one agent, lost in the middle of the primordial jungle.

Some agents could lock themselves away in a vacant cubicle, work there, survive there, and die there, without anyone ever seeing their face or hearing their voice. The invisible agents were the exception to the rule of office operations, because it was so hard to hide for any length of time one's presence in the corridors and to protect one's cubicle from assaults.

Maybe he had kept his story to himself all this time, or maybe he had already told it to others, who listened with a distracted ear and quickly turned on their heels from the dangerous novelty he represented.

He said his name was Piotr, and that's pretty much all we knew about him.

There were so many other questions to ask him that we simply forgot to ask who he really was. Or maybe we didn't really care, just as we don't care about all the rest, about who the others are, what they do, what they think, and what they feel. Taking an interest in others, no matter the reason, is in any event a dangerous undertaking, and we have acquired the reflex to refrain from doing so. First, so as not to risk attracting attention, but mainly to prevent anyone from taking an interest in us. Because talking about ourselves, revealing things about ourselves, opening the doors wide to who we are, are all breaches in our intimate fortifications that our enemies would exploit to eliminate us.

It was Théodore who first spotted Piotr, who discovered him.

According to what he told us, it was his mystical calendar that told him he should go to the west window that night, on a part of the floor we never visit. It is home to the Scarlet Brigade, which we had nicknamed thusly because of the colour its cubicles take on in the evening, when the rays of the setting sun transform the cloudy sky into a glowing blaze that shines on the corridors and the walls. The Brigadiers have always lived in hope of conquering the cubicles along the west window. Other guilds have always tried to prevent them, such that screams, battles, and fanatical chants often ring out from this part of the office. For the Brigadiers, who have been fighting for so long, the completeness of the Scarlet Brigade has evolved from a strategic challenge into a religious ideal. The west window is a dangerous, violent place, and it would be foolish to go there without good reason.

But Théodore did not discuss his calendar's orders, and at the 21:00 break, shortly before nightfall, he made his way as far as the glowing red corridor to station himself facing the sky, waiting for a sign, unaware of what form it might take or what it might mean.

He saw bodies fall past the window, agents smiling with their eyes closed and clothes billowing with the velocity of the descent, accompanied, like a bride and her train, by a procession of glass fragments twinkling in the dusk, voluntarily defenestrating from the floors above, deciding to see the street for at least a few tenths of a second before crashing into it.

Théodore didn't pay any attention. There was nothing unusual in the suicide ballet, and it provided rhythm to the scenery, like a frequent, benign meteorological event. No one was moved because, plunging to the ground at a great speed, the bodies were no longer agents, but hunks of flesh with no cubicle, no future. How can you be moved by a hunk of flesh? How do you identify with it and imagine that you could meet the same fate? The suicides that continually streamed by on the other side of the tall windows were nothing more than bloody drops of a foreign rain. The only thing Théodore felt in seeing them was annoyance that they were disrupting his contemplation of the sky.

It was just when he thought he recognized in a cloud's shape the face of a man he once knew that Piotr cracked open the door to his cubicle.

In a split second, Théodore leapt against the wall of the cubicle, slipped his hand through the crack, twisting Piotr's shirt collar to drag him to the ground.

'Are you a Brigadier?' Théodore asked his strangled victim, who was pinioned by a leg lock.

'In the beginning, humans were born on the ground,' Piotr answered.

This sentence sounded so strange in the hallway of the west gallery, vibrating to the sound of the laments of the Brigadiers, that, out of surprise, Théodore released his grip.

He sat down on the dirty carpet while Piotr caught his breath.

'What?' Théodore asked.

'In the beginning, humans were born on the ground,' Piotr repeated. 'The carpet was green, not blue, and they called it grass.'

Théodore glanced at the window. He searched for the face of the man in the clouds and, no longer seeing anything, concluded that it wasn't the sign he was waiting for.

He stared at Piotr again.

His sign was here, indoors, in the form of Piotr bathed in the burning glow of the evening, huddled on the worn carpet, with

40

grey hair, deep wrinkles, a sickly body, its bones no doubt weakened by age, including those of the hands under the skin, like children in adult clothing.

Piotr was the sign that his calendar had asked him to find.

'We can't stay here,' Théodore said. 'Let's get back into your cubicle before a Brigadier finds us.'

During the next break, at around half past twelve, we were gathered in the bathroom, not quite knowing how Théodore had managed to convince us to break a fundamental rule of survival by occupying a common space after sundown.

'I'm sure there are cameras watching us,' Laszlo said. 'We're going to end up on the street because of your nonsense, Théo.'

'There are no cameras,' Solveig said calmly. 'Why would they install cameras when they can just make us believe there are cameras?'

'Because there are lunatics like Théodore and like us who don't give a shit about the rules,' Laszlo said. 'That's why. You don't think they know? You think they think we're sheep?'

'Shut up, everyone,' Théodore said, interrupting. 'Listen to Piotr. If my calendar told me that I should find him, it means we're not risking anything.'

'Stupid imaginary calendar,' Laszlo grumbled. 'Your goddamn calendar is going to get us killed. I'm outta here.'

Laszlo headed to the door, but stopped short when Piotr repeated the sentence that would be the start of his story.

Laszlo immediately forgot that he had just announced his departure. He said nothing more and, like us, listened to Piotr's story in silence, for a long time, while, in the office plunged in darkness, our bodies grew cold.

# 8.
# THE STORY OF THE MILLENNIA
# BEFORE US

'In the beginning,' he says, 'humans were on the ground. They were born there, crawled there, and died there. It was a dark time, when distances stretched out in every direction and, like the lives of these beings, space itself didn't have a horizon.

'The entire globe was a curved cubicle that savagery demanded be shared in repugnant global promiscuity.

'These beings were called humans, but today we call them cats, because deep inside them roars the animal, and little distinguishes them from the animals that we have now ceased to be.

'In the beginning, humans were born on the ground, and the carpet was green, not blue, and they called it grass, just as they called the corridors streets, and the cubicles houses.

'In the beginning, humans were born on the ground, and for millennia they tried to share it, by putting up walls, installing fences, carving stones, marking lines, noting anything that could tell them what belonged to whom, so that ideally everyone would be separated from each other.

'It was the long, harsh work of humanity, work that lifted it up from the magma of sweaty bodies to the pure verticality of today, that changed potential into being and possibility into certainty.

'In the beginning, humans lived on the ground, and it would be a long time before all the surface area was distributed among those who had chosen solitude over community.

'At that time, wherever you looked there was space. As strange as it may seem, humans believed it was practical not to live where they worked and not to work where they lived.

'So, in the morning they rose to go to a place that was used only for work, then in the evening travelled the same route in reverse to sleep in a place that was used only for that. The money they earned from working enabled them to pay for transportation, food, and a dwelling to sleep in. This is why they were called not agents but employees. They had no agency. They were employed.

'It took a lot longer for the rivers of employees travelling from one unnecessary place to another to peter out. Some understood the absurdity of the situation; others simply no longer had the means to pay for a place they used only to sleep. The prices of the cubicles they called homes became so high that only companies could pay for them. Companies, not needing to sleep, and therefore not needing a place that served only for that, divided these homes into offices and moved their employees in.

'In just a few years, the world that had been divided was divided again, between companies that could pay for it. On the ground, they built new offices; these offices were divided into cubicles, and in these cubicles, they housed agents.

'When, finally, there was no more space on earth to build new offices, the world started to resemble the one we know.

'It was at that exact moment, when the last human gave up the last house and, having become an agent, was relieved to go into a cubicle in an office, that the ground where the humans were born was no longer the ground. At that exact moment, it became the street, everything that wasn't the office was the street, where all there was to do was die, where all there was to do was to live like cats, which amounted to the same thing. On the one hand, the offices, and on the other, the street. This was how the world was separated and organized, obeying an obvious logic that had managed to escape us up to that point.

'So, the street became a fable. No one left the offices anymore, because there was no point, and so no one knew what the street and those who live there had become, if indeed there was anything other than cats living there.

'In the beginning, humans were on the ground, but no longer. Finally, everyone lived in dignity and walked on fresh carpet; we forgot that the ground was green and that it was called grass.

'At the time, the earth was divided into a finite number of offices, themselves divided into a finite number of cubicles, but this arithmetic became problematic, with the number of agents far exceeding the number of cubicles available.

'Decent people found themselves on the street, fighting the cats for sustenance and their lives, battling the winds, feet in the muck, railing against the injustice that decimated them in the open air, while others, no better than them, died in the warmth of a cubicle, satisfied and fulfilled by a life of work.

'At that moment in history, the world could have crumbled, broken into pieces by disappointed masses, vindictive hordes of out-of-work agents, snarling day and night against a system that seemed not to want them.

'At that moment in history, the world could have crumbled, because businesses could not immediately see why they would have to employ new agents, because those who already populated the cubicles had nothing to do anymore, nothing to build, design, or await.

'The automated world was already in place, and machines worked for everyone. Being an agent, even in those times, involved occupying a cubicle and pretending to be working. It was on this faith that one acquired dignity and the esteem of one's peers and others.

'And yet, at that moment, the world could have crumbled, torn apart by those who felt ashamed, who felt like cats, who had in some ways become them. Their violent bitterness could have swept away in one night what had been built.

'To avoid the world of humans sinking into chaos, announcing the advent of the era of cats, they made the two final decisions of the old world.

'This ushered humanity into an era of progress, dignity, and work that is the era we know today.

'The first decision flowed from the desire of every human to raise themselves up from the ground. Starting from the carpet of a global ground floor, humans gave themselves over to vertical logic and took possession of the final dimension of which they had not yet become masters.

'On top of offices were erected other offices, and on top of those new offices, still others. The number of cubicles multiplied by as many storeys as gravity would allow. From a flat universe, spread out on the ground, the humans' buildings themselves stood erect. All decent people that circumstance had thrown to the street could then become decent agents, because, everywhere on earth, offices went up that, from that time on, were called towers.

'And the more the towers grew, the less the hordes screamed, and, even when they did, the height of the buildings prevented anyone from hearing them. Ground floors were sealed off; no one wanted to be on the ground anymore.

'When the earth's attraction prevented them from erecting one more storey over the last storey, they knew exactly how many cubicles the world contained, and therefore how many agents the cubicles contained.

'And to avoid new tensions, and new risks of destruction, they made the final decision of the old world.

'In those times, humans still engaged in the vulgar reproduction of cats. There was no longer any advantage to be found in it. Misshapen women were often forced to stop working and, for months, plunged into the shame of idleness, while men, disturbed by the chemistry of their animal bodies, trembled with fear and temptation, feeling themselves becoming cats again, which they no doubt still were a little. Worst of all, it had become unbearable to many agents to waste endless hours training the offspring created this way.

'The final decision of the old world was therefore mathematical. It involved establishing the number of agents that would populate the world forever.

'Procreation like cats was forbidden, and they created institutes where machines would be better than anyone at training offspring who would become replacements, without wasting the time of agents busy working.

'And so, a replacement would be assigned to every cubicle freed up, such that the number of agents would never exceed the number of cubicles.

'It was the final decision of the old world and the final decision of all possible worlds, because the new world thus created became the ideal that we know today.

'This story is the story of millennia that came before us. It explains how humans overcame, through work, the obstacles that lay before them, how they stopped sleeping where they didn't work, how they organized the world so that everyone works, how they renounced the ground to stand tall, and how they separated the office from the street, how they left chemistry to cats, and how, freed of these constraints, conquerors of the scourges, survivors of the shame, they could finally exist with dignity; from then on, their only activity, made of dignity and passion, wisdom and reason, was to work.'

AGENT IDENTIFICATION:
SOUTH QUARTER \ TOWER 35S \ 122ND FLOOR \
Y1 SECTOR \ CUBICLE 314 \
FEED: LOCAL NEWS \ 04:52


## URGENT NEWS

Following the discovery of a broken pane in the west window of your floor and the disappearance of Agent Piotr from cubicle 45, located near that window, we remind you that defenestration is strictly forbidden in tower 35S, whether voluntary or caused by another.

Offenders may be subject to legal action for the following reason: damaging company property.

An investigation was opened to locate the perpetrators of the offence and reached a finding of suicide for the above-mentioned Piotr.

We remind you that in the event of voluntary defenestration, for whatever reason (suicide, a game, etc.), costs for the repair of the destroyed pane will be charged to all agents who occupy the floor of the deceased agent.

Finally, we remind you that suicide, regardless of the method employed, is strictly prohibited by Paragraph 1 of our Labour Code.

– 8-Char


## GENERAL NEWS

The automatic repair of the broken pane in the west window was postponed by six hours to allow agents who knew Agent Piotr to pay their respects. It is temporarily permitted to throw some of his personal effects through the opening of the west window.

We request that agents from neighbouring cubicles not interrupt this tribute and excuse any possible drafts or drops in temperature.

# 9.
# THE CURRENT EXISTENCE OF
# A MOSQUITO

'You are going to lie on your back, like this.'

She has taken off her clothes, is standing over him, covered only by adhesive strips that hide her sexual attributes. Purple grooves wind their way between what look like bandages, scarred memories of past adventures, reverse stigmata, an inversion of a tradition in which wounds are the marks of a saga. In her case, the injuries are the saga, the wounds the adventure, every bite of metal a new victory over the stubborn permanence of her body. As she talks, she looks in the mirror that covers one wall of her cubicle and sees how her scarred flesh changes colour, each point of impact giving her skin a different hue. These unevenly sized marks spread like paint on a canvas, combining with other marks to create new hybrid colours, brilliant pinks, dark blues, green highlights, a silent moan from her beleaguered immune system. The intermingling shapes drawn on her skin create a map with no landmarks, long scars barely healed in mountainous relief and craggy chains rising above anonymous seas and deserts. If I must be here, she always thought, if we must carry around with us this flaccid thing that itself drags along our purposeless thoughts, let this thing be beautiful. Our permanent pain, the despair planted in our back like a traitor's letter opener, let these appear on the surface of our body, let them be the banner of our disgust at being alive, and let our flesh never find rest, let the suffering make it sag, so no one ever imagines we are happy, or carefree, not even us.

'First, I'm going to inject this.'

She takes a syringe from the desk to her left and can't quite supress a grimace of sad compassion at the sight of the fine, clean, sparkling syringe, already filled with anaesthetizing liquid, a metal messenger tube, strategic bridge between the battle on the outside and the battle on the inside, that gently pierces the epidermis, the dermis, and then the hypodermis, a windowless train that watches the quiet cells go by.

Clara lifts the pant leg of the man lying on her desk and plants the needle in his thigh, which draws from both partners a more resonant exhale than our daily breath.

'Mosquitos are creatures of the perpetual past,' she says. 'They feed on the blood of vertebrates, planting their microscopic proboscis into our flesh in a penetrating, discreet relationship. Since they go to the trouble of anaesthetizing us with their anticoagulant saliva, we don't feel anything in the moment of the act. It's only later, when the anaesthetic encounters on its route our natural chemical defences and the invisible jousts of this battle start to itch, that we become aware of the bite and the theft of blood it is testimony to. At that moment, the mosquito is already long gone, full of our blood, which, at thirty-seven degrees Celsius, warms and intoxicates them. When we feel the bite of a mosquito, we are attesting both to its existence and its absence in the here and now, holding only one certainty deep inside us: it was there. This is why mosquitos are creatures of the perpetual past: a past certainty, a current probability.

'No one says, "A mosquito is biting me." They always say, "A mosquito bit me."'

'There is nothing to prove that the insect that has bitten us is still alive when we feel the bite. The buzzing we hear in the cubicle could very well come from an animal other than the one that carries and is digesting our blood.'

'Why are you telling me this?' the man asks.

She slowly pulls the needle from his thigh and smiles.

'Because you are having the opposite experience. The bite you felt on your thigh is already a memory, it is a probable past, which will be certain only if time and pain prove it to you. The anaesthetic I injected into you will take effect, and the pain will disappear along with your other sensations, and for your body this bite will no longer exist. Even the memory of the needle will be uncertain, because the memory of your thigh will be as well.'

Her gaze drifts beyond her own reflection, a fuzzy, shapeless mass that she refuses to recognize simply because it is there.

'When we don't feel anything anymore, when there is nothing to indicate that we exist, it's pain that allows us to be sure. Some fight and suffer for it. Others stay shut away, working to exhaustion, to find the pain and its constant memory. But you and me, we have this bite, this liquid, and these tools to remind our bodies that we are alive, that we aren't dead machines like the ones that educate and manage us. Being alive, knowing it, and suffering because of it, that is our gift, beyond even the torture of work, which will end up becoming sweet because we are incapable of finding anything else to do.'

'I can't feel my thigh anymore.'

'It's strange how we start to become aware of ourselves and our value as soon as it starts to vanish. You never thought so much about your thigh until you could no longer feel it. We do this to prevent you from forgetting about yourself completely. Believe me, when I'm done, you will never forget that you have a thigh, and maybe one day there will never be a single second when you forget who you are, what you are made of, and what you are doing here.'

'I don't really know what I'm doing here.'

'Trust me, I will remind you.'

And Clara takes a scalpel, her face registering no emotion.

She plunges the blade not far from the spot where the anaesthetic was administered.

She cuts the flesh of her colleague, whose name she still doesn't know, but whose tissue she now sees opening, his severed vessels bleeding, offering his insides with resistance.

Once she has finished – opened, lacerated, and then folded back the skin, made deep incisions and others more superficial, like a painter mixing pigments on a palette – she will sew up her partner with threads of different textures and diameters, so that the scarring is not uniform, producing controlled colours, crevices, and protrusions.

Then the two agents will go their separate ways, and it will only be much later, when the anaesthetic wears off, that the agent will understand what Clara was saying during the operation, and that, writhing in pain, he will think back without being able to prevent the nagging buzzing of a mosquito whose current presence cannot be proven.

# 10.
# THE ANNUAL SHOPPING SPREE

Thinking about the blood on our hands is unproductive. Getting lost in a labyrinth of guilt is also unproductive.

Thinking, motionless, about the form the present could have taken if our actions had been different is an activity that keeps us away from what we are for too long to allow ourselves to surrender to it.

And so, none of us alluded to Agent Piotr in the grey aftermath.

Work resumes. The numbers accumulate.

The sky grows dark. Lights come on. Constant clinking from the cafeteria spreads through the office.

Communications are limited, movements are made only if they are necessary.

The atmosphere is heavy, a taut wire that we fear will break at any moment.

It's a middle of the month like any other.

At 14:31, the office sinks further into silence.

The midday break in the middle of a month is a critical moment. The same way Théodore reads the crucial moments of his existence on a fanciful calendar, agents fear the hurdles, the changes, the symbolic hours and dates they don't see, that they are not warned of, but that they sometimes feel simmering under their damp skin.

The midday break in the middle of a month is one of those moments that are so red that they turn black, jammed into the empirical calendar we have all decided to follow, driven by an aware-ness of the evidence and the force of experience.

Ordinarily already silent, the office then sinks further into obliv-ion, as if life no longer inhabits the cubicles, and, abandoned to bacteria and amoebas, the world itself calmly crumbles, the towers melting under the methodical action of erosion, our flesh decom-posing into a rich humus, the dust of our bones mixing with the dust of the offices in ruins.

Not one breath disrupts the moaning of the wind that comes in through the window Agent Piotr went through.

The company protects us. It takes care of us. It wants well-being and the greatest possible longevity for its employees.

This is why the company fears these moments of utter tension, when a spark can send a sector, a floor – maybe even a tower – up in flames.

It is often in the middle of the day in the middle of the month that the company offers us an annual shopping spree, to substitute harmless inactivity for our dangerous lack of activity. It distracts us, for a few crucial minutes, from the piece of quartz, so we won't see what is glittering before our eyes.

The numbers disappear from our multi-dimensional screens.

The event is important enough to stop everyone from doing anything disruptive.

Attentively monitoring the messages from the company is an important rule, and anyone who breaks it knows the risk.

At 14:32, a familiar face appears. It's Douglas Beekle, the company's shopping host.

His appearances are eagerly awaited. It's the only time of the year when agents can enhance their comfort by investing in new equipment for their cubicle. New equipment means better protec-tion, increased value, and a rise in power of one sector or guild.

These shopping sprees are also the only times agents can use their credit, aside from the mandatory and automatic purchase of food at the cafeteria.

But, today, no one suspects the revolution that is brewing.

When Douglas Beekle starts listing the equipment available in the global store – ergonomic backrests for our reclining chairs, undetectable, microscopic q2 cameras to mount on the walls – every agent opens their blank notepad screen and carefully enters what they can afford, barely listening to the descriptions of the objects that are beyond their investment capacity.

'This revolutionary material,' says Beekle, 'was designed at the request of many agents to respond to the armour-piercing bullets we brought you last year. If your cubicle walls are equipped with this type of armour, no known projectile can reach you. Laboratory tests show that its rate of resistance exceeds that of a standard armoured wall by 500 per cent. In other words, a cubicle protected by the new Titan5 metal is impenetrable, for the low, low price of 6,999 ecus.'

A weary sigh can be heard throughout the floor.

The calculation takes no time at all.

To shell out 6,999 ecus, an agent must have occupied a cubicle for around thirty years and spent those thirty years buying nothing but food and water. You can count the number of agents who meet these criteria on one of Théodore's feet.

Douglas Beekle smiles and goes on.

'And now for this year's big news, which I'm sure will delight all of our colleagues. Our banking experts have just given us the green light to modernize our system for assessing the solvency of an agent. While no one has complained, the company was aware of the inflexible terms for bank loans. The system for calculating the life expectancy of an agent based on the location of their cubicle, whether it looks onto an aisle or a window, was not only unfair, but it didn't encourage mutual support either. Yet, as you know, the company believes that solidarity is the key to collective success. Therefore this will be corrected.'

Douglas Beekle stops talking, and a confident smile spreads over his face while a colourful title appears on the screen, accompanied by booming music.

'I present to you the Solidarity Loan!'

The logo spins, flits, and shrinks until it settles in the upper right-hand corner of the image. The volume of the music drops, Beekle fades out, and graphics and illustrations take his place in the foreground to illustrate the terms of the new system.

'That's right: thanks to the Solidarity Loan, a guild can now take out a loan in its name and pool the productivity potential of its members. It's the life expectancy of the guild and not its agents that determines the size of loan granted, which could extend longer than the life expectancy of all the agents of the guild in question. You're not dreaming: now you can buy things you wouldn't have been able to pay for in your lifetime! On one condition. To be eligible for a Solidarity Loan, a guild must meet this requirement: its members must occupy adjacent cubicles.'

A rumble of consternation rises up in the office. Aside from the Scarlet Brigade, which concentrates its objectives for conquest on a specific part of the office, guilds are not territorially minded, and the cubicles of their members are scattered throughout the floor, which ensures their safety. This is the case for our guild. None of our cubicles are located in the same sector.

'As you can see from the examples shown, the Solidarity Loan offers more incredible possibility the greater the number of adjacent cubicles. The borrowing power of each cubicle is not just cumulative; it multiplies depending on how the cubicles are arranged and where they are located. A guild that holds an entire sector of eight cubicles can borrow the maximum amount, which would exceed five hundred years of repayment and give it funds of around a hundred thousand ecus, even more if the sector is in a good location. And what could make more sense, after all? Until now, when one of you unfortunately leaves us, your replacement benefits without having spent anything on the improvements and equipment you leave behind. Does that seem fair? The Solidarity Loan rectifies this injustice. It offers you more freedom, more purchasing power, and it emphasizes what we care about most, both the company and you:

solidarity. The details of this new offer will be available on the intranet any minute now. This shopping spree will end in exactly twenty-four hours. Happy shopping, and see you next year.'

Beekle's smiling face disappears and is replaced by the store catalogue.

At the same time, keyboards throughout the office start to clatter. A seasoned agent knows that the excitement is more than just consumer hysteria. On the contrary: everyone is discussing, analyzing, and formulating the new strategies required by this upending of the rules.

Our guild is no exception.

# 11.
# THE LAST CUBICLE

The words run together on the screens, hiding the lines of capital we are supposed to be monitoring that announce the collapse of a company somewhere far away, where thousands of agents are suddenly thrown onto the street, having settled for what we are all settling for.

Our guild's discussion circuit is closed, sealed to other agents. No one wants to weigh in publicly on the offer that Douglas Beekle has just made.

The guilds are abuzz, a silent buzz that hides their fear and excitement about the event.

Our words overlap and superimpose in no order, and, despite our routine, we are surprised, at times, to see that we don't know who is saying what; words are broken down into piecemeal thoughts in constant movement, swirling in the fibre optic cables of the internal network, in a flow of pure, spontaneous emotion, in a flow of information to sort through. The discussion channel has become the guild's buzzing brain, of which each of us is only a negligible nerve cell, working to make an entity larger than ourselves function, the guild becoming an individual that exceeds and controls us, without a leader or a throne. Each of us both organ and limb, eye and hand, slave and master of our collective and individual destiny. Our guild comes to life the second it gains the right to borrow money.

[chan#9926] THÉODORE: You have all taken leave of your senses. Have you forgotten that it's the middle of the month?

[chan#9926] LASZLO: We don't even know whether the middle of the month still means anything.

[chan#9926] LASZLO: They have changed time into space. What used to be minutes and seconds has become square metres.

[chan#9926] LASZLO: Middle, beginning, end. All that will be forgotten. What counts now is the equipment a cubicle has.

[chan#9926] CLARA: No equipment will replace a full pay packet and our power. The power of our purchases is more important than our purchases.

[chan#9926] LASZLO: Prices have already gone mad. The balance of power is reversing. What had value now has less. The have-nots can become invaluable.

[chan#9926] CLARA: It's only temporary. Prices will stabilize. What counts is not what we buy, but what we can buy.

[chan#9926] SOLVEIG: Are they inciting us to war or peace?

[chan#9926] LASZLO: The company doesn't think about what works for us. The company sets rules that favour its own expansion.

[chan#9926] THÉODORE: But its expansion depends on us. If we engage in open warfare, we will be less productive.

[chan#9926] CLARA: Or the company planned this war and thinks it's necessary for greater stability in the long run.

[chan#9926] SOLVEIG: But there's no war!

[chan#9926] LASZLO: There will be one.

[chan#9926] LASZLO: A war for power.

[chan#9926] LASZLO: For purchasing power.

Something became clear to us right after Douglas Beekle spoke, but clarity doesn't justify acting hastily.

We have to talk, debate, discuss. The guild can't start anything without the unanimous consent of its members.

The hive mind vibrates with the contradictory thoughts of each person, so that the final choice is everyone's choice, without being the choice of just one.

[chan#9926] LASZLO: Piotr's cubicle is a priority target.

[chan#9926] LASZLO: The Brigadiers will want it to fulfill their ridiculous prophecy, but it is also located in a sector that has seven cubicles held by the Bookies guild.

[chan#9926] LASZLO: If they understood what Beekle just said, they will try to take possession of the remaining cubicles so they can take out an enormous Solidarity Loan.

[chan#9926] LASZLO: Before even attacking the Underlins who live there, they will move on Piotr's cubicle.

[chan#9926] LASZLO: We have a card we can play.

[chan#9926] THÉODORE: It's madness!

[chan#9926] THÉODORE: Our guild is puny.

[chan#9926] THÉODORE: It is powerful in defence, not attack. That's how we're organized.

[chan#9926] THÉODORE: Never face-to-face combat. Fleeing in style is better than death. Have you forgotten?

[chan#9926] LASZLO: Everyone knows Piotr is dead. Everyone is waiting for a replacement to arrive.

[chan#9926] LASZLO: But no one saw us. The guilds are feeling around in the dark. They know that someone got rid of Piotr, but they don't know who. That ignorance is our ally.

[chan#9926] SOLVEIG: Some people think that Piotr killed himself. Some think the coast is clear.

[chan#9926] LASZLO: Only an idiot would think Piotr ended it himself.

[chan#9926] LASZLO: We can handle idiots.

[chan#9926] CLARA: None of the guilds are afraid of us.

[chan#9926] CLARA: Not the Bookies or the Copiers.

[chan#9926] CLARA: And certainly not the Scarlet Brigade.

[chan#9926] LASZLO: No one needs to know we were behind Piotr's death.

[chan#9926] THÉODORE: So, who was then?

[chan#9926] SOLVEIG: On the west window side, it could have been a Scarlet Brigade operation.

[chan#9926] THÉODORE: You want us to pretend we're the Scarlet
    Brigade?
[chan#9926] THÉODORE: We're all going to die.


When we threw Piotr out the west window, it wasn't in a bid to
gain territory.

We didn't talk about it afterwards, because deep down we didn't
know exactly what had driven us.

It wasn't anger or hatred. And it wasn't fear either.

It must have been destiny, and logic. Even Piotr didn't do
anything to stop us. He just accepted the obvious.

You couldn't talk the way he talked, reveal what he revealed,
and keep working as an agent. Piotr knew it. We knew it. That's why
he didn't make a move that night when we grabbed his arms and
legs and threw him with all our might through the window.

Now the cubicle is vacant. It is equipped. No debt is attached to
it, and its location is highly strategic, along the west window. This
makes it an invaluable asset, and the replacement who takes possession
of it will be coveted by many forces. Either to make him an ally or to
kill him and wait patiently for the end-of-month replacement.

[chan#9926] LASZLO: We will attack. We will seize the cubicle. And we
    will train the replacement who moves into it.
[chan#9926] CLARA: We'll have to move quickly. Piotr's memorial has
    given everyone time to reach the same decision.
[chan#9926] LASZLO: We will watch, wait, and stand ready. When the
    replacement arrives, we will protect them.
[chan#9926] THÉODORE: We don't have the power that takes.
[chan#9926] LASZLO: We won't need it. As soon as someone tries to
    attack them, we will make people believe that the Scarlet
    Brigade –
[chan#9926] THÉODORE: It's suicide.
[chan#9926] CLARA: Sadly, no.

The bodies of William and Sandra Vinière, the late CEOs of Chicago West Inc., will be destroyed by vitophagous bacteria on Sunday, on the roof of tower 97N in the North Quarter, in keeping with their final wishes. The compostable matter disintegration ceremony will be officiated by Cily Vinière, their only daughter and the sole heir of the west zone of Chicago 3, according to the funeral rites of the parish of Aries. Many international personalities and the couple's friends and colleagues are expected for the event.

William and Sandra Vinière were found dead on Tuesday, at their home in the 6N tower of the Nacre Quarter. An initial investigation has found the cause of death to be poisoning from toxic fumes from the chemical toilets 25 floors below. A fault in the tower's switching module accidentally inverted the flow of treated air and that of gases from the fecal matter of agents from tower 6E. According to Humbert Chan, a specialist in the chemistry of decomposition, the quantity of toxic molecules found in the Vinières' apartment was more than 1,200 times higher than the acceptable rate for a human organism, and this high rate seemingly caused the couple's death less than 26 seconds after the technical problem.

This is the first accident of this kind ever recorded in the history of the modern world.

Switching modules are found in all human towers. They control the flow of hot toxic gas generated by the decomposition of fecal matter. Some of it is reinjected in the treated air of towers, both for heating and to reduce the amount of gas released into the atmosphere. The system has never failed before, and the technical investigation should determine if such an accident falls under Fung's Law on converging factors, or if major work should begin on all human towers.

# 12.
# THE REPRODUCTION OF CATS

On the image delimited by the camera's viewfinder, two white masses separate, two incandescently white bodies, which expand with the rhythm of their breathing. The office is plunged in darkness. The only source of illumination is a round light bulb, a globe of light hanging in the centre of the image.

The camera is rolling. The two agents catch their breath. Black dots start to fly around them – flies attracted by the dampness and the salt of their skin. The insects disrupt the quiet of the moment. The two agents stand, pick up their clothes, and start to get dressed.

LASZLO – Don't worry. No one will know.

SOLVEIG – I know.

LASZLO – If I use the images or sound, or if I just use what we have done as material for art, no one will believe this really happened. Agents don't believe anything anymore. All around us there are betrayals, strategies, and manoeuvres, so everything that is said, everything that is heard, sometimes even everything that is seen, is no longer considered truth. None of us believes anything anymore, not even our own eyes or the slash of a blade. Some agents, when they are dying, keep on working, doubting even their own pain, their own death throes – their own death.

SOLVEIG – I don't care, Laszlo. Do what you like.

LASZLO – You're not afraid?

SOLVEIG – What do I have to be afraid of? Being fired?

LASZLO – It's a possibility. We've violated article 20. If someone finds out, we'll be thrown onto the street.

SOLVEIG – I won't give them time to do it.

The agents don't look at each other.

Solveig finishes putting on her cotton jumpsuit, then turns out the round light bulb. The camera adjusts its focus and brightness. The scene is now bathed in the first blue light that the window lets in every morning in this part of the office. Laszlo approaches the lens. His face takes on gigantic proportions, and his voice is deafening when he starts talking.

LASZLO – You worry me, you know. It's like you're trying to get fired.

SOLVEIG – I'm not trying to do anything. I'm settling for doing what needs to be done. What else can we do?

LASZLO – I don't know... Hope.

Solveig laughs. Laszlo points the camera at her. He zooms in. His colleague's smooth face fills the image.

SOLVEIG – You're funny. Sometimes, when I listen to you, I feel like you're fresh out of the institute and that you still don't understand what we're doing here. Hope is dangerous for agents, Laszlo. You can distract yourself, write your novel if that's what you want, but it's a big risk to hope that that, or something else, will take you anywhere other than where you are.

LASZLO – Do you think everything we're doing is only a distraction? While we wait...

Solveig looks down and stares at something on the desk where a few minutes ago she was sitting, eyes wide open, hands gripping Laszlo's shoulders while he penetrated her and they engaged in the bestial practice that the laws of agents prohibit. Laszlo points the camera in that direction and zooms in. Four flies are enjoying a few drops of blood. In a close-up, we see the proboscises of the insects plunging with delight into the brown liquid.

Solveig opens a drawer and takes out a spotless handkerchief that she stares at just as long. Then she answers, while wiping up the blood – the flies have flown off.

SOLVEIG – I think so, yes. And I'm sure the guild thinks so too. We came together around the idea. If anything sets us apart from other agents, it's definitely not hope. It's just our desire to use the time we are given to make humans more human. A fight against ugliness, a fight for perfection. But, like any fight for an ideal, it's a battle that's lost in advance, that holds no hope. Only pride, lots of pride, and a minimum of integrity.

LASZLO – You change your appearance like Clara. You remove all your hair. You do this for the others, to become your own message.

SOLVEIG – No. It's for me first, then for the guild. I have nothing to prove to anyone else My search for perfection has nothing to do with them.

There is a long silence, and a tiny familiar vibration spreads through the office.

The generator has come on. It must be 04:30.

Solveig throws the stained handkerchief in the recycling airlock. Laszlo zooms in and once again the image is an extreme close-up of her.

LASZLO – What we just did, Solveig, is the opposite of perfection. We did what cats do. We listened to our inner beast. We forgot we were humans tonight. I knew I would do it one day. That was my plan. One of my plans. I never imagined that I would do it with you. Now you are even more of an enigma to me. I don't get why you did it. I don't get what you want.

Solveig, who was still half smiling, suddenly grows dark. Now she stares at the lens. Her emotionless eyes, without eyelashes or eyebrows, form two chasms in the smooth oval of her bald head.

SOLVEIG – When you advance with your head bowed on the road to perfection, when you know there is still an end point to reach and there always will be, sometimes you want a stain. The desire to become nothing, a soulless object brushed aside by destiny with nothing more to do. You want to be dirty, as dirty as you can, the least human, the least alive. You want to be disgusted by yourself, vomit on yourself, heap shame on yourself. Every day our imperfection wraps us in this profound despair at being almost nothing. We tell ourselves that, since we are dirty, humiliated, raped, violated, bruised, lower than low, as detestable as a cat, each step that will follow can only improve us and bring us closer to an unattainable ideal. We need that stain to deal with our imperfection. That's what I felt when we were doing it. Pain, shame, and the tragic abandon I had forgotten the taste of. Now, for me, this endless shame that seeps from my pores like a film of sweat is a new mountain to climb, a new ordeal to overcome, that will lead me for a few days, a few years, to the dizzying fall of a new humiliation. But, at least during the climb, I feel like something is changing in me, and that from the worst I am heading toward better.

Laszlo slowly zooms out. Solveig shrinks. The walls of her cubicle, then her desk, return to the image. Laszlo backs up as far as the door, leaving Solveig in the centre of the frame. Then, suddenly, the image melts, dissolves into a monochrome painting. The video becomes a graphic animation, Solveig becomes a drawing, and, brutally, her sketched silhouette plunges into the recycling airlock, following the bloodstained handkerchief, going straight into the vacuum tube, crushed by the cylindrical duct, broken down into millions of thready pieces by the microscopic jaws of the grinder on the mezzanine, the remains of her pulverized body instantly assailed by legions of vitophagous bacteria, reduced to increasingly small molecules, reconstructed in new chemical bonds, to end as beneficial mineral dust, fertilizer spewed outside by a spluttering bellows. The image lingers on one of these particles, a tiny black dot that flutters in the wind, under the ceiling of grey clouds. As far as the eye can see, other towers rise up, populated by other agents. While the movement accelerates and the particle returns to the tower, sucked up by another duct, rushing through a stylized network of tubes and hoses to wind up expelled from the system by a huge fan. The particle has returned to the office. It floats, it falls gently from the ceiling, and in falling it grows bigger, it takes human form. It lights up. Its silhouette and its features become more defined. It's Solveig, in her white jumpsuit, who sets down where we left her. The sketch fades and, imperceptibly, the video image reappears.

LASZLO – That's it exactly, Solveig, what I call hope.

# 13.
## THE 8-CHAR DOOR

In the office, there is a door.

Our cubicles are armoured, our locks are unpickable, and our walls are bulletproof, but nothing we have can rival the impenetrable materials of that door.

The door is a passage, a step, and a frontier between what is and what isn't.

We call it the 8-Char Door, but as is often the case, it's a name without history or objective meaning, the way Théodore is called Théodore and Solveig Solveig. Like the words that are used to name us, the 8-Char Door is a combination of syllables that allows us to differentiate it from the other doors in the office.

All those who now live on this floor arrived through the 8-Char Door, and most who leave will go through it again.

It's the only physical connection we have with the company, and that is why everyone both respects and fears it.

When our last name, at one time, appeared on the admission screen of the institute, we walked through an identical door, crossed the threshold, and found ourselves plunged into darkness. When the light finally returned, it was the greyish-white light of office fluorescents that the 8-Char Door had just opened to reveal. Our career started on this threshold. The indescribable fear that plagues us every day is the fear of being forced to end it at the same place, rather than dying peacefully of old age in the warmth of our cubicle.

Walking through the 8-Char Door the other way leads to one place, and that place is the street.

The 8-Char Door is an airlock between the before life and the status of agent, and between work and the status of cats.

The 8-Char Door can give life and it can take it away. Even though it is a mere door, it regulates, organizes, and constrains the flow of agents on the floor.

There is never any sign that the 8-Char Door will open, no warning light, no siren, but after years spent awaiting death in this office, everyone instinctively knows the time it takes between the demise of an agent and the opening of the door that will reveal their replacement.

Usually, the event is too trivial to notice, and the replacement has to find their way to their cubicle alone, knowing only the number. But today, despite the penetrating calm of the office and our over-riding obligation to never stop working, it is obvious that all eyes are glued to the door and the young employee who is going to appear in its opening.

The replacement who is arriving and who, right now, sees their name displayed on the light panel, takes a last look at the blue-and-white walls of the institute, then walks toward the door, happy and proud to have been chosen to become the adult they were dreaming of becoming and who will move into Piotr's cubicle. Our eyes, those of the Columnists, those of the Bookies, and maybe those of other agents who belong to other guilds, are therefore glued to the door. It is 16:45, and already time is on our side. If the replacement had emerged during a break, the welcome committee would have barely allowed them the time to get to their cubicle, and we wouldn't have had the power to intervene. Our plan would have misfired. But, since we have to work, no one can make a move before the 17:45 break. If the replacement is receptive, an hour is all it will take to get them to grasp their importance and get them on our side.

Since the announcement of the Solidarity Loan, gossip is circulating in the aisles, rumours are making the rounds of the mystical intranet, typed between the lines of trivial discussions in which a shrewd mind can detect a second, coded language. Plans are being assembled; strategies are taking shape. The trepidation is so strong that, getting up, sliding our noses above the walls of our cubicles, sniffing the office air, we smell the aroma of tension that precedes an attack. It's the smell of battle, of new power, as if all the agents on the floor can't stop their bodies from producing sweat and adrenaline, warning pheromones that drift from the cubicles, whirling close to our nostrils before being absorbed by the tower's ventilation system and released in such concentration that other towers in the city may also be on alert, not knowing why their offices are suddenly filled with fear and anticipation. The entire city may be trembling and fearing the danger of imminent combat, saturated in our scent and our fragrant message as it envelopes buildings, taken up by the wind, causing other agents to secrete the same olfactory messages, which then add to the thick fog of fear in which the whole world may now drown.

On our floor, at this exact moment, skirmishes are already taking place, but no attack has been mounted: wasting energy in the middle of the month would be ridiculous. The only thing at stake in the office for now is Piotr's cubicle, the only free one, the only one that justifies taking risks. There are two possible strategic approaches to it.

It would seem that some guilds plan to immediately kill the replacement who walks through the 8-Char Door in a few seconds. Kill them, or set traps that will have them out on the street right away. Having gotten rid of them, they will do it again with the next replacement, and likewise with the next one, until the end of the month.

This strategy has proven effective in normal times. But this time the tactical data has been turned on its head. Other guilds, like ours, have chosen protection and will deploy every means possible to ensure the crucial replacement is not taken away. Gaining their trust by intervening, showing them that, without us, they would already be dead, making ourselves indispensable and valuable, that is our strategy, and it requires a demonstration of force, the intimidation of attackers, to avoid armed conflict at all costs.

It is 16:47, and a faint noise emerges from sector A1. Everyone holds their breath.

The sound is the perfect gliding of the 8-Char Door rolling along its track. At 16:47 today, the 8-Char Door reveals a young man who appears, everyone agrees, quite old.

# 14.

## A RATHER OLD YOUNG MAN

Hick appeared in the 8-Char doorway like a sword pulled from its sheath, propelled by a disturbing assurance, with no regard for the icy breath of looming danger.

He crossed the office, from sector A1 to the west window, whistling a happy tune. His fingers snapped to the beat. In his wake, the cold gust of his impertinence chilled all who heard the refrain.

Either he is very clever, many agents thought, or he is the stupidest replacement we have ever been sent.

Yet the replacements were trained – relatively little, but nonetheless trained – over the years spent at the institute, in the dangers that would lie in wait for them in the world of the agents. None of them arrived here oblivious: everyone was aware of the need to keep a low profile for long enough before taking the risk of moving about in the open.

Hick was wearing a purple tunic with a high collar whose flaps fell back to his chest, and underneath one could glimpse a white shirt embroidered in lace and purple velvet pants cuffed at his ankles. His hair was long, black, and shiny like the barrels of our guns.

Clara was photographing the young man, taking advantage of the location of her cubicle, one partition of which looked over the central aisle and another the corridor that leads to Piotr's old cubicle. She sent us the images one by one on our guild's secure network. We were paralyzed, as we had been a few weeks earlier in discovering our friend lying in her own blood on the tile floor of the bathroom.

Once again, the private war that divided our consciousness had broken out, its two generals finding in Hick, his unusual attire, and his suicidal attitude a perfect act of war. On one side, it was unbearable for us to see our only hope for survival squandered so openly, given the small chance he had of lasting even a few days in the cynicism and violence of the office, while, on the other side, we were fascinated by his original clothes, his obvious taste, and his casualness that was confidently unaware of the laws and norms we had bent to for so long, combatants for beauty, decidedly, but slaves to the rules that ensured our low profile and safety.

The clothes we were wearing were the same as those we wore when we came through the 8-Char Door. Every replacement selected at the institute chose, from among millions of combinations of colours and shapes available, the uniform that would be theirs the rest of their lives. An agent cannot change their appearance. It's an immutable law of the office, which we imagine is intended to conserve, somewhere in a global agents file, a faithful description and a photo that will never be out of date.

Barely adults, shaped by the institute, how could we have adopted anything other than the most banal, the most understated, the least showy of uniform? How could we have, with the first choice that was ours to make, decided to stand out, and in doing so take the insane risk of becoming a target, when we had barely arrived in the office?

No one ever took the risk. That is why all agents dressed the same, in an invisible grey, three-piece suit, with a white shirt and a charcoal tie. Some women would deviate from the rule and wear a cotton jumpsuit, the colour of which ranged from pristine white (like Solveig's) to inky black (like Clara's), with infinite shades of grey between.

[chan#9926] THÉODORE: Clara, could you adjust your camera a little?
There are shadows on his face.

But Clara didn't answer and left one of us to explain the source of the mysterious fine lines that streaked the replacement's face.

[chan#9926] LASZLO: Those aren't shadows. They're wrinkles.
[chan#9926] THÉODORE: What? Just how old is the replacement? How is this possible?

No one answered, obviously. No one knew what was going on. We settled for continuing to watch him as he almost skipped down the most dangerous aisle of the office, in the heart of Scarlet Brigade territory, merrily humming as if he were walking through the Vinière clan's synthetic gardens at Chicago 3, gardens of peace and calm that we saw pictures of on the open general news channel.

'Ah, this must be it!' the newcomer said loudly once he got to the armoured door of his cubicle.

[chan#9926] CLARA: I can't decide whether it will be harder or easier with this maniac.

Clara said the words we were all thinking in one form or another.

Then the office jumped when the wrinkled young man shouted at the top of his lungs over the partition walls of the cubicles: 'Hello, everyone! I'm your new colleague. My name is Hick!'

He had literally yelled. And this time, no one bothered to express the thought that went through all our minds at once. The answer to Clara's musing was obvious. With this sort of maniac, there could be no more doubt: everything had just become considerably harder.

# II.
# CAUSALITY

## IMPORTANT NOTE

You are reading the news channel during work hours.

The company reminds you that such activity is authorized for only three minutes a day.

As a result, the news below has been summarized to allow you to read it in the time available to you.

## PERSONALIZED NEWS

The sun has been up for 54 minutes and 02 seconds. Were it not overcast, it would already have shone into your cubicle.

You are Agent Élisabeth. This morning, your mood is mixed.

You have agreed to bonus overtime, which extends your workday until 01:15, and you are having doubts and misgivings.

Nevertheless, the stars in the third house of Taurus confirm that you made the right choice, and it will serve you throughout your career. Stop worrying and persevere in your duties.

The company thanks you for your efforts.

## GENERAL NEWS

Like all your colleagues on the 122nd floor, you were upset and perhaps alarmed by the arrival of the replacement named Hick.

As a strict directive, the company recommends that you avoid interacting in any way with the new arrival. The company recruited this agent with full knowledge of his many qualities and is now working to correct his faults, which are known to 8-Char. Until this operation is complete, the company encourages employees on the 122nd floor to keep their distance from Agent Hick and above all not to put stock in anything he may say. If, despite this, you were to talk to this agent during a break, the company asks you to make our efforts easier by reminding him as firmly and as often as possible of the rules that govern the office and the consequences of an infraction.

# 1.
## SHORT-HAIRED CATS

We are managed by machines.

They create us, raise us, and guide us our whole lives.

They allow us to eat, to be housed, and to work.

The machines embody perfection. They think better than we do, operate better than we do, and no one has ever considered questioning their superiority. The agent, by nature, is a creature on a quest.

Physically, spiritually, and intellectually, the agent is an imperfect hybrid whose characteristics swing between the vulgarity of the cat and the perfection of the machine, which operates tirelessly, without pause or question.

The machines are the perfect image of what every agent aspires to, the formidable and ultimate image that serves as an ideal and a role model. And if, today, within our particular guild, we continue to place importance on art, a shameful, subjective activity, far from the rigorous impartiality of the machines, it is because we are always fighting the cat within, directly, without claiming to be anything other than a body that sweats and bleeds, a short-haired cat whose pupils shine in the night.

This intimate relationship, a combination of envy and fear, that we have with the machines takes the form of thought patterns.

We would like to be them, and, to get closer, we strive to think like them, developing in our heads programs in their language, which is so pure and precise, we are but condemned the rest of the time to forging opaque concepts that the pitiful shapelessness of our language forces us to endure, perplexed, speechless, unable to untangle the possible from the certain.

We hate our language, and our words, and the murky ideas they produce, because office life does not tolerate imprecision, and here there is no acceptable risk. The slightest error could see us thrown onto the street, so to our eyes nothing excuses this terrible handicap that hobbles us and exposes us to error. Our language is a burden, an open wound in our side that constantly threatens to kill us. This is why we are secretly working to abandon this language, and these words, and these amorphous ideas, which bring us only the shame of not yet being machines, and of remaining these pathetic embryos mired in their unfinished genetic code, not knowing what to do about it except to feel sorry for ourselves, imperfect, about this other thing we could be.

This is why, when a problem arises, all our discussions, which can be conducted only in the language of agents, are merely dirty curtains that barely let through reality, while elsewhere, in white rooms, bright spaces, our thoughts try to design in the language of machines clear programs that when executed will lead us to the truth.

In these planes illuminated permanently by the sun, the constants and the variables line up into blocks surrounded by parentheses and brackets. If the problem is simple to solve, our brain arrives at a solution and we smile gently, proud of this outcome that has momentarily changed us into a machine. Yet, often, the complexity of the computational engines we develop prohibits us from accessing secrets without the help of computers, and, with shame gripping our guts, we are forced to deliver to our perfect allies the mathematical food that their nanoscopic entrails will digest until the interrogative raw material is transformed into a diamond of immaculate certainty.

The machines generate us and raise us.

And, nourishing in us constant humiliation, the machines guide us, our entire lives, and give us answers that our deficient nature would never have allowed us to glimpse.

# 2.
# IN OTHER PROBABLE UNIVERSES

As astonishing as it may seem, no guild tried to approach Hick during the 17:45 break.

Many agents had nonetheless identified and displayed on their screens supposedly infallible tactics, plans, and predictions. The powerful simulation software had noisily hummed in the hearts of the closed cubicles, carefully evaluating assumptions and conjecture, to finally spit out, from the guts of pure science, meaning and method ready to use. The fretful agents had welcomed these lines of results like pilgrims at worship, ecstatic before these hyper-rational prophecies, endless rows of probabilities, each one calculated based on thousands of random factors.

From potential armed opposition down to folds in the carpet, every imaginable variable had been included in the attack algorithm, a bouquet of interlacing curves, the outcome of which – noted as 'objective' in the program of probabilities – for some required enlisting the young replacement and for others executing him, pure and simple.

Chaotic compositions, tissular tapestries of mathematical subject matter in a language of metal, these cold-blooded evaluations had coiled, like snakes, their long tail of digits after the decimal on the desks of probable and, therefore, powerless assailants.

if
(infinite rows of possibilities, $A_1$, $A_2$, ... , $A_x$)
then
{infinite rows of instructions, $C_1$, $C_2$, ... ,$C_{x-1}$}

With Hick's arrival, black spittle fell on the flurry of immaculate predictions and now dripped and stained the perfection of possible futures.

No computer or software could have predicted that this would be the day when, through the 8-Char Door, not a replacement, but Hick, would emerge, an enigmatic creature hiding in his brain incredible, undefinable, and opaque matter. Madness, idiocy pushed to extremes. Or worse yet: a dangerous ability to understand faster than us the stakes of the office, its dangers, and its secrets.

No one could confirm either of these hypotheses, and neither could the machines, which is why the program that predicts future events was hanging, in a loop, in every cubicle, on the same unsolvable problem.

```
if (Ax == Hick)
    {
        {
        if (Hick == crazy)
            then instruction Cx
        }
        {
        if (Hick == idiot)
            then instruction Cy
        }
        {
        if (Hick == genius)
            then instruction Cz
        }
    }
```

Logically, it was not these specific variables that made the combatants – including us –stand down, but the utter inability to choose between the three, when the hour struck and it was time to execute carefully studied strategies to seize Piotr's cubicle.

'We have to do something,' we read on the guild's closed network. No one paid attention to the sender or to the wisdom of the words.

And so, against all expectations, nothing budged at 17:45. While at the same time, in another space-time dimension, where the replacement who appeared at 16:47 was not Hick but someone else, everything exploded and died, and litres of blood spilled on the walls of cubicles amidst the cries and whimpers of warriors, and the bulging eyes of the young person who had barely arrived rolled back in their head, forcing them to regain consciousness fast enough to ward off the next attack – a spray of sharpened metal – lethal ricochet of self-propelled projectiles – avoided – dodged only to discover a new threat approaching, missed them again – one – then another – saved by the sacrificial member of a guild who had preferred to charge straight toward death rather than letting it claim their protégé – until the next one – an attack from the rear – or from above – depending on the dimension they were in that didn't contain Hick – without interruption – battle – inhuman – feral – cat fight – appalling but necessary – until the liberating climax – and peace.

Nothing budged at 17:45, except for Hick himself, yelling to anyone who wanted to hear that he was happy to join such a beautiful family of agents and that he would be delighted to have coffee with a new friend near the cafeteria – or some other insane provocation.

Still nothing budged at 21:00, and when the 00:15 break came, and some of the agents stopped working while others continued to monitor the smooth operation of the infallible machines for an hour of overtime that would earn them a few extra ecus, nothing budged either, not here, not in another space-time dimension, not in the supposed parallel universes, on this specific day at this specific time; in the universe where we work, no one made a decision, and, in other universes, regardless of the replacement who had come through the 8-Char Door instead of Hick, the replacement was dead, their flesh and bones dissolved by the acid clouds, and calm was restored in the office.

This is how all the possible universes, at this exact moment, were plunged into silence, regardless of the reasons that led to the quantum bifurcations and the birth of these realities without Hick.

Few agents visited these divergent realities. Despite the certainty that permeated them, all agents risked having regrets and therefore imagining what would have happened if a tiny variable of the equation of their own life had been different, imagining how much this variation would have transformed the present. And so, our present wasn't this exact moment stitched here and now, but the hazy superposition of all the possible presents. Its overall structure remained unchanged (an office, a job, a cubicle), but tiny anomalies differentiated one possible universe from another. Anomalies, or details, but nothing fundamental. These possible universes that straddled our own had the advantage of resembling each other in substance.

What was new here in our world lay only in a negligible and infinitesimal deviation in the groundswell that carried us toward the future. Not toward the futures, but toward the only future of agents, modelled on the rigour of the machines, the most powerful of which we assume had everything planned so that nothing would hinder the march of humanity toward verticality in all its glory.

This is why, when in dreams or daydreams, we visit one of these parallel universes – 'universes with green carpet' or 'universes where we ate rutabagas at noon' – it ends up breaking down on its own, too similar for us to want to linger. And if we got the foolhardy idea to leap into a universe that is radically different, the life we led there, the horrors that occurred there, and the misfortune that afflicted us made us shiver or quickly open our eyes: we are indeed here, in this office, at this precise moment in history when everything is good for everyone.

Somewhere else, after all, could only be worse, and few agents felt the need to convince themselves of that, even in the imagination.

# 3.
## THERMODYNAMIC DEDUCTION

All night, unable to make a decision, none of the guilds approached Hick's cubicle. Not the Scarlet Brigade, not the Bookies, not even us.

We didn't sleep. We didn't talk. We barely thought, imitating the machines tired of running an unsolvable equation.

In the shadows, we observed the metal pillars that kept our cubicles upright and thought about the physical forces at work in preserving this immobility.

We were these metal cubicles, objects of uncertain solidity, immobilized by two forces: the gentle attraction of the earth and the resistance of materials that make us up. With stronger attraction or weaker resistance, we could have been pulverized or ejected toward the grey sky.

We dreamed we were tightrope walkers, elements assembled from a stationary system at the centre of which the constants were fixed. Deep down we felt reassured not to move. Not to crash to the ground. Not to be sucked up toward the heavens.

All night, we stayed quiet. We didn't disrupt the integrity of the system with our movements, thereby subjecting ourselves to the laws of physics and thermodynamics learned at the institutes, which helped us accept our powerlessness in the face of the new piece of data that had just jammed our equation of attack.

The case of Hick presented a simple problem of thermodynamics. Which is why the machines had not solved it. The laws governing our stable world prohibited it. And an intervention to seize Piotr's cubicle ran the risk of destabilizing the global system.

No machine or agent could flirt with that possibility. Despite our battles and warlike acts, it was unbearable to imagine that the office could disappear, order could evaporate, or work could not get done.

Physically, we lived in a confined space. The laws indicated that this unique, closed system was fragile. Without an exchange of energy with the outside environment or another system, the slightest disruption risked provoking complete disorganization. As such, it became possible that the known world would enter an endless spiral of chaos.

It was to avoid this universal chaos that the machines hushed up. And so did we.

The morning had come, the hot plates hummed, and the screens displayed the usual personalized news.

A workday was beginning.

The present took hold of us again.

At 08:50, as the workday was ticking by and agents were struggling to forget that they were even more pathetic than the night before, a message appeared on the guild's private channel.

[chan#9926] LASZLO: It's a mistake to do nothing.

No one answered, and a few seconds passed.

Agreeing with what he said was illegal.

Claiming that something else could be better was not against the law, but actions developed on this basis could be.

So, we waited for Laszlo to develop his thought.

[chan#9926] LASZLO: We and the machines are trying to preserve the integrity of the system.
[chan#9926] LASZLO: We think acting would challenge order and stability.

[chan#9926] LASZLO: But we asked the machines the wrong question, because we assumed that, even after Hick's arrival, the system had remained stable.

Some of us frowned and approached the screen.
We were starting to understand.

[chan#9926] LASZLO: But it isn't anymore.
[chan#9926] LASZLO: The disruptive element in the system is Hick, and any effort to channel his energy will help restore stability.
[chan#9926] LASZLO: Doing nothing is a mistake, because doing nothing preserves nothing.
[chan#9926] LASZLO: Doing nothing leaves the system to disintegrate and plunge into exponential chaos.
[chan#9926] LASZLO: Not acting is what's dangerous now.

The proof was obvious. Of course, it was hard to accept that the institute had placed a disruptive element in the office. And yet the morning news clearly said that the agents should support the company in putting the not-so-young Hick back on the straight and narrow.

[chan#9926] LASZLO: Hick is a problem. And a threat.
[chan#9926] LASZLO: The company knows it and wants us to act.
[chan#9926] LASZLO: The company is counting on us.

The local news for the 122nd floor was contradictory, and it didn't seem like the company to wreak havoc in this way. On the one hand, it was prohibiting us from spending time with Hick and, on the other, it had enjoined us to guide him onto the right working path.

Since the company never made a mistake, there was only one explanation for this apparent uncertainty. It was a veiled order.

In openly asking agents, which is to say guilds, to take Hick's fate in their hands, the company knew it was formalizing a war that was already threatening to break out. The company did not encourage or authorize war or combat in the office, ever. At best, it tolerated what went on and considered losses necessary to balance the system. But officially recognizing that agents had the right to attack others would change the very structure of our organization, which was directed toward a single objective: work. The sole goal of breaks, as we experienced them, was to allow our organisms to regenerate so we could get back to work refreshed. Under no circumstances were we officially authorized to do anything other than rest or feed ourselves during these downtimes. That morning's news, we understood it better now, was to spur us to action, while the prohibition to act remained in place. If this was the case, we had to draw one terrible conclusion: Hick was indeed a threat to our office.

And, as a result, to our work.

# 4.

## RUNNING THE RISK

At the 11:15 break, we gather in front of Piotr's old cubicle, and our eyes, unconsciously, avoid lingering on the window at the back of it, even though our ears are lashed by the tinkle of glass shards colliding in the air before being scattered over the office carpet.

We regret nothing but prefer not to think too much about what we did, out of fear of having to regret it.

The plan was organized on our discussion channel during the morning, and everyone knew what they had to do.

Everyone had to go into the cubicle to meet Hick, but only Solveig would negotiate with him. Meanwhile, Théodore would stay in the corridor, in front of the closed door, to bar access to it by other agents who might have drawn the same conclusion as us. To thwart these possible competitors, Théodore was instructed to pretend he was part of the Scarlet Brigade and that Hick had contacted him. Those who tried to approach would understand that the war was over and that attacking Hick was now an attack on an entire guild, with all the consequences of that act.

This ruse, while dangerous for us, is a last resort, the final recourse if Théodore's presence is not enough to drive away the assailants.

We knock on the door of the cubicle while watching the area.

We hear someone moving around inside, a drawer closing, a throat clearing, traitorous sounds that Hick will soon learn to hide.

Finally, the door opens to reveal Hick's face.

'Welcome!' we all say at once, careful not to shout our simulated enthusiasm too loud.

Hick is speechless, then he cracks a wide smile.

'Ah!' he says. 'Here you are! I thought no one was ever going to accept my invitation! Not a lot of laughs around here, are there? You guys need to loosen up a little!'

We look at each other, closed expressions on our faces, and Solveig does the talking, like we had planned.

'Hello, Hick,' she says. 'And on behalf of our guild, welcome to the office.'

She holds out a small gift package we had put together a few minutes earlier.

Hick opens his eyes wide with emotion and places his right hand on his heart.

'Goodness,' he says, a sob in his voice. 'You shouldn't have. That's so lovely.'

Théodore stamps his feet behind our back. In part because his amputated toes prevent him from keeping his balance, but also because we are gathered in the corridor, at the mercy of a camera that enemy guilds would waste no opportunity to point in this direction.

'Not at all,' Solveig says. 'It's nothing. The first day is never easy for replacements.'

'Yes,' Hick answers. 'Particularly when it's the second!'

He bursts out in a booming laugh that stiffens the spines in attendance. Surprised by the power of the laugh, Théodore almost topples forward, but a last-second pirouette stops him from crashing into the partition wall of the cubicle across the way. He regains his balance and is stoic, when Solveig puts an end to this dangerous situation.

'Can we come in?' she asks. 'We don't want the other employees to see your gift. Rumours travel quickly, you know.'

'Oh, of course. How rude of me. Come in, come in. It's not very big, but we should all fit.'

Solveig gets ready to go in first but stops. Stooped, she hangs on to the door frame.

'Thanks again,' Hick says. 'You shouldn't have!'

'Not at all,' she stammers, suppressing a hiccup. 'It's...'

But Solveig doesn't finish her sentence.

She falls to her knees and vomits on the greyish carpet of the corridor the solution – a mixture of tea and carbonaceous organic matter served in the cafeteria – used as fuel for agents in a hurry.

'...nothing,' she utters through translucent spit, tears in her eyes, before our crestfallen faces.

We know that under no circumstances should we deviate from the approach protocol, and no one dares say anything. Solveig is our spokesperson, and even though her capacities are obviously diminished, we don't try to intervene, except to help her up and support her while she enters Hick's cubicle, with us on her heels.

Clara closes the door behind her with a nod in Théodore's direction, as if to say, 'Everything is fine, she can do it.'

'What...um...,' Hick stammers. 'What do we do for the carpet?'

Solveig wipes her eyes with her forearm, indicates that she will answer once she catches her breath.

'Don't worry,' she eventually says. 'The company will make you pay for the carpet cleaning, because it happened in front of your cubicle, but we will reimburse you.'

'Ah,' Hick settles for saying, visibly relieved. 'Well then... Welcome to my cubicle.'

We force a feeble smile when the replacement looks at us.

'Can I open it?' he asks Solveig, who will be the only one doing the talking, something he must have understood.

'Of course, of course,' Solveig says.

Hick takes a letter opener out of the drawer and uses it to carefully peel the tape from the gift.

He unwraps a varnished wooden box with a golden clasp.

'What is it?' he asks, excited.

Solveig makes a superhuman effort to smile at him, and we notice that she seems to be tormented by another hiccup.

'Open it,' she says. 'You'll see.'

'Oh!' he exclaims, a little too loud for our liking. 'Tea! That's so thoughtful of you!'

'We know what it is,' Solveig says in a quiet voice, as if to let him know it would be a good idea to imitate her. 'When you arrive in the middle of the month with no money, you need a little something in your stomach at the end of a day.'

She suppresses a burp and almost loses her balance. Right behind her, Clara holds her by the shoulders so she doesn't collapse on the floor.

Hick laughs. 'I would have preferred a roast pork with shallots, but I can make do with this!'

Hick's joke garners only embarrassed giggles, while Solveig, in a bad way, seems to be fighting an image that has just formed in her mind.

In this image, she has left the cubicle. She can't see Hick anymore. She can't see us anymore. She is not even in the present. She is in the future, or the past. At the 14:30 break, in any case.

She is in sector M1. The sector with the cafeteria, standing in the line of agents who are awaiting their turn to order a meal from the vending machine. She feels her stomach gurgle and calculates approximately how much time until her turn. Not long. It's now. On the backlit keypad of the vending machine, she frenetically enters the code for a succulent roast pork with shallots. She looks through the smoked glass of the machine and can make out the nanorobots busying themselves with assembling, from carbon reserves and basic items stored in the tower, the dish she has just ordered. The nanorobot ballet gradually reveals the roasted meat, the fatty sauce, and pink shallots arranged prettily on a large white plate. The vending machine emits its characteristic clink. The cloud of nanorobots vanishes through the vent duct, and the service hatch opens onto the steaming meat, the strong aroma of which fills her nostrils. She grabs the dish and, without waiting to get back to her cubicle, hungrily takes a bite, licking the piping-hot sauce she feels coating her chin.

Then she lifts her head and sees that Hick and her colleagues are staring at her, frozen.

She is on all fours on the ground and, plumb with her head, a puddle has covered the carpet.

She squints and can see in front of her, she could swear, in the shimmering liquid, a single molecule of theine struggling to float and that, helpless, is reduced to pieces by an armada of famished enzymes. She sees the chemical bonds break and almost hears the molecule scream, shredded, decomposed like she herself will be someday, under the effects of time and vitophagous bacteria, reduced to a gaseous state and primordial matter, stored in billions of fragments of itself in the tower's storerooms, waiting with no awareness of time to be assembled again by a multitude of nanorobots in the cafeteria vending machines on some floor or another. She sees the atoms combine, the carbon accumulating in a few seconds, and this molecule that was a piece of her take its place in the overall arrangement decided on earlier on the machine's backlit keypad. She sees the molecule, the infinitesimal part of her that, despite her own death, has survived her. She sees it incorporate itself, with so many others and in appalling promiscuity, to the already finished organic structure. She sees this molecule, this primordial fraction of what she is, ideally integrated into an overall whole. And that overall whole is the roast pork with shallots that Hick has just ordered from the cafeteria, because he loves it, and because he is alive, and if he is alive, it's because she is there, on all fours in his cubicle, trying to save his life.

She cannot suppress a violent spasm and vomits again.

\#

Cily Vinière, the new CEO of Chicago West Inc. and sole proprietor of the west zone of Chicago 3, has just announced she will visit all facilities she is at the head of to collect any complaints from agents under her authority.

Given the scope of the undertaking and Ms. Vinière's limited free time, interested employees will soon be asked to draft short, clear requests and send them to a company-designated representative. The representative will put together a summary and submit it to Ms. Vinière when she visits facilities.

This unique initiative, to the new CEO of Chicago West Inc.'s credit, should not be understood by agents as questioning the system or any part of the system introduced by the people of our times. On this, Cily Vinière said that she was committed 'not to consider attempts to destabilize the working world,' and to 'immediately report any complaints that suggest that the employee making them could disrupt the future operation of a given company.'

Ms. Vinière's tour will start in two weeks, and the full schedule of her visits will soon be available on the global network of Chicago West Inc., in the Management Agenda section.

\#

Milton Banks, honorary actor with Akzion Studios, announced today in a recorded press conference that he will accompany Cily Vinière on her visit of the west zone of Chicago 3, making official his relationship with the new CEO of Chicago West Inc.

This statement ends more than a month of suspense during which outlandish rumours circulated on different channels of many competing companies. Despite this slander campaign, Chicago West Inc. and Akzion shares shot up 13 and 9 points respectively in the past 30 days.

'This happiness has visited us at an unusual time, and I am proud to be at Cily Vinière's side to help her recover from her recent tragic loss,' Milton Banks said.

# 5.
## HOW HE AGED

At the institute, children learn to read feeds.

It's their only activity, but it is absorbing and complex enough to keep them busy throughout their years of study.

Later, when they become agents, their duties will essentially involve monitoring millions of pieces of data that scroll by on their screens. Among the shapes and colours continually bombarding their retinas, they need to know how to distinguish what is normal and what is not. That will be their job.

Early on, child apprentices must integrate the signs, codes, and languages machines use to describe the complex movement of the modern world.

To optimize their learning, students are evaluated through simple tests every sixty minutes. The slowest are moved to a room suited to their abilities, while the more quick-witted ones are oriented toward higher-level teaching machines.

This approach means that not only are each student's abilities developed as best they can be, but their perpetual mobility prevents them from being distracted by possible conflicts between them. These constant reassignments through the different teaching rooms are a taste of the dynamics of the office they will eventually join, also disrupted by arrivals and departures, associations and ruptures, where affinity between agents is more often a handicap than an advantage.

During this initial training, students are encouraged to show initiative, creativity, cunning, and autonomy, while fatigue, laziness, and chatter are quelled with class demotions. Nevertheless, and despite the constant reassignments, the effectiveness of the teaching machines allows child apprentices to emerge from the institute with a negligible age difference between them, generally just a few months. In stepping through the 8-Char Door, a replacement invariably has smooth skin, fear in their eyes, and an intact face.

From as far back as we remember, we have never seen a replacement join the office who was as old as Hick, who appeared strong, experienced, and surprisingly sure of himself.

During our first conversation, even though we didn't have much time, Solveig asked him the question.

It was years ago, he answered, and it was a misunderstanding.

While, generally, every question had an answer in the teachings of the institute, young people were also sufficiently overwhelmed with information that it wouldn't occur to them to ask anything, nor did they have time to think about anything other than what they were being taught.

The refrain of instructors could be summed up with these words: 'Your question will be answered in a later class.'

What the machines taught us formed a coherent whole. Our entire world, uniform and efficient, was described in the slightest detail. The only grey zones or imprecision an apprentice could detect in a course would be systematically clarified in the next one. Far beyond how to read capital feeds and colour codes for critical economic situations, our education gave us to understand, from an early age, a single, sole truth, from which all others flowed: the machines are infallible.

Hick quickly acknowledged this reality and did not argue with it. But his analytical mind and extraordinary memory had nonetheless prompted him to voice serious reservations about some of the truths he had been presented with. So, unlike his classmates who were also told that their question would be answered later, Hick never forgot his question, not to be subversive, but simply because, even as a child, he wanted answers, and the certainty of the machines was not enough for him. Deep down, his goal was not to reach a particular truth or to fault the machines, but to understand why they were trying to hide an aspect of the functioning of our world. In our world, which Hick also deemed perfect, and the functioning of which was the result of thousands of years of research, trials, and pain, in our world where everything was designed to make each person's existence as beautiful and pleasant as possible, what could be so sensitive, he wondered, that they would refuse to talk about it to the young apprentices?

There was nothing about Hick that seemed disruptive. Like all of us, he believed in the system, in the glory of work, and the need to devote oneself fully to it. But Hick refused to accept that part – even a small part – of our perfect reality was hidden from him.

When the instructors had first alluded to the street and the condition of cats, the apprentice couldn't think about anything else or settle for the fragmented description he was offered.

From that moment on, while the other apprentices quaked in fear at the mere mention of the street, Hick did not stop bothering the system to find out more on the topic. He kept coming back to it, regardless of the topic of the lesson, paraphrasing, using metaphor, images, each time coming at the question from a different angle, without appearing to, but single-mindedly, until one day, tired of instructors' silence and vagueness, he decided to explain his point of view. He reconstructed for us word for word what he had said that day.

'We have no contact with the street.

'Even on the lowest floors of the shortest towers, the fog is so thick that we can't see what's going on there.

'But we are taught to make statistics our weapons and our shields. We are told that percentages and numbers are our allies and will be throughout our lives.

'And yet, statistically, an agent who accidentally falls from a window has a slim chance of survival… But there is a chance. So, what happens to them?

'We were taught how our body is designed, how it fights illness and injury, how we scar and form new cells every second.

'What if that agent did survive, miraculously get up, and visit the street?

'What would they find?

'Who would they meet?

'Those who were fired?

'Because a lot of the fired employees are still alive when, dismissed from their duties and banished, they go through the 8-Char Door and the company ejects them from the tower.

'What do these shameful elements that work itself has rejected do? They must walk, touch, and see. They don't stand around waiting for a radioactive gust to contaminate them. They must try to survive. Even without work. Even reduced to the condition of cats, even less worthy than the threadbare chairs on which agents sit, they must have to search for food and get organized, in some way or another, as pitiful and pathetic as they may be.

'Maybe there is a life down below, a society, even a civilization, that eats, sleeps, and thinks, that reproduces like cats, but that reproduces regardless.

'These repulsive children produced by detestable parents grow up without ever knowing work, or at least the glorious work of agents.

'These men, women, and children who must be there, down below, regretting not being able to participate in the incredible momentum of human civilization, what do they know? What do they think? How do they live without the machines?

'Maybe, despite it all, they have awareness and hope. Maybe they are embarrassed and disgusted not to be more useful than the cats of this world. If that is the case, maybe they are already working on elevating themselves. Maybe they are even building machines that can guide them through the twists and turns of the dark future spread before them. We can't remain in the dark about these inferior peoples. We have to be concerned about them, we have to know exactly who they are and how they live.

'Maybe we already know.

'Maybe there are cameras that can pierce the fog and microphones pointing at the ground, and maybe, somewhere, in a tower, agents are busy monitoring this world beneath the world. Listening to the voices of people who have become cats that crawl. Analyzing the movements of numbed hordes, thrown to the unfavourable winds.

'It would be logical and important. And just as important that we know it. And unfair that we don't know it.

'It is impossible that the machines, in their perfection, left this detail out. They must know something, probably everything. But then why not talk to us about it? Why let us imagine when the truth exists? Why let us be afraid when there is obviously an explanation? And why leave those people there, down there, if there are any? Those who have been thrown to the street, it's understandable, but the others? Those who fell? Or those born on the ground? Why let them sink into the horror and shame of being nothing more than a cat?

'And, most importantly, what exactly is a cat?'

This endless question had earned Hick a measure that we didn't even know existed: the complete isolation of a student. Without receiving an answer or taking the periodic sixty-minute test, he was asked to leave the class immediately and go into an empty room with a personal instructor on one wall. Proud and eager to receive an answer, Hick did not need to be asked twice, but, as he explained it, the isolation room was not a reward. It was a punishment. And that punishment lasted a few years, during which Hick never saw another child or a room other than the one where he had been taken, no other instructor than the one he had been assigned.

He spent endless days in solitude and silence, learning non-stop, always executing the same tasks and subject to the same hourly tests that were now for nothing. And yet, thinking that this isolation was a test of his patience and determination, every day he asked the same question, in the same terms, hoping they would end up answering him and congratulating him for having been so tenacious in his quest for truth. Every day for years that he had given up counting, he got up in the morning, learned, asked at noon what he ended up calling 'the cat question,' learned in the afternoon, and went to bed in the evening without receiving an answer.

We were silent as we listened to this story, in the face of Hick's incredible pugnaciousness, but once he had finished, Solveig laid a hand on his shoulder and softened her voice to ask him to confirm what we had already guessed.

'If you're here, it means you stopped asking the cat question?'

Hick's face lit up. 'Not at all, I asked the question just yesterday. But rather than answering, "Your question will be answered in a later class," like always, the instructor said nothing. A few minutes went by, and I had the impression that the entire system was restarting or shutting down. The door opened onto the common room. I saw my name on the light panels of the exits.'

We looked at each other, in silence, not needing to say that, with Hick, we were making one of the best acquisitions in the guild's existence.

What stood before us was the only human stubborn enough to have pushed a machine to its limits.

# 6.
## THE VISIONS AND THE LIE

[chan#SQ8837] SOLVEIG: It's not the first time I've had that sort of vision.

[chan#SQ8837] LASZLO: You don't eat, Solveig, so it's hardly surprising.

[chan#SQ8837] LASZLO: The more you deny yourself, the more your brain fantasizes about food.

[chan#SQ8837] SOLVEIG: But I've never vomited before.

[chan#SQ8837] SOLVEIG: It's dirty.

[chan#SQ8837] LASZLO: We aren't machines; we're humans.

[chan#SQ8837] LASZLO: And humans are dirty.

[chan#SQ8837] LASZLO: They are so dirty they invented dirt.

[chan#SQ8837] LASZLO: Without humans, there might not be what humans call dirt,

[chan#SQ8837] LASZLO: but there wouldn't be anyone to call it dirt,

[chan#SQ8837] LASZLO: so maybe it wouldn't really be dirt.

[chan#SQ8837] SOLVEIG: Spare me your reflections.

[chan#SQ8837] SOLVEIG: I don't want to be dirty.

[chan#SQ8837] SOLVEIG: Not like that.

[chan#SQ8837] LASZLO: You talk about dirt because it's the only thing that's important to you.

[chan#SQ8837] LASZLO: And that scares you.

[chan#SQ8837] LASZLO: But, deep down, if I heard you right,

[chan#SQ8837] LASZLO: you saw Hick eat you.

[chan#SQ8837] SOLVEIG: It wasn't me.

[chan#SQ8837] SOLVEIG: It was a molecule.

[chan#SQ8837] LASZLO: A molecule that was you.

[chan#SQ8837] SOLVEIG: A molecule.

[chan#SQ8837] SOLVEIG: That's all.

[chan#SQ8837] LASZLO: Are you afraid of Hick?

[chan#SQ8837] LASZLO: You think we made a mistake in recruiting him?

[chan#SQ8837] SOLVEIG: Hick is seeking the truth.

[chan#SQ8837] SOLVEIG: We are seeking beauty.

[chan#SQ8837] SOLVEIG: It is unlikely we will get along.

[chan#SQ8837] LASZLO: And why is that?

[chan#SQ8837] SOLVEIG: You know very well why.

[chan#SQ8837] SOLVEIG: You want me to spell it out for your stupid novel.

[chan#SQ8837] LASZLO: So, spell it out.

[chan#SQ8837] SOLVEIG: We won't get along because

[chan#SQ8837] SOLVEIG: beauty can't handle the truth.

[chan#SQ8837] SOLVEIG: A large part of beauty resides in the fact that it sustains silence

[chan#SQ8837] SOLVEIG: and lies.

[chan#SQ8837] SOLVEIG: Seeing everything,

[chan#SQ8837] SOLVEIG: saying everything,

[chan#SQ8837] SOLVEIG: understanding everything

[chan#SQ8837] SOLVEIG: is the opposite of beauty.

[chan#SQ8837] SOLVEIG: Truth,

[chan#SQ8837] SOLVEIG: to be precise,

[chan#SQ8837] SOLVEIG: kills beauty.

[chan#SQ8837] SOLVEIG: It transforms everything into the equal of every other thing.

[chan#SQ8837] SOLVEIG: It brings the ugly and the beautiful to the same level,

[chan#SQ8837] SOLVEIG: the just and the unjust,

[chan#SQ8837] SOLVEIG: good and bad.

[chan#SQ8837] SOLVEIG: In the eyes of truth, one true thing is equal to another true thing.

[chan#SQ8837] SOLVEIG: There is no hierarchy to truth.

[chan#SQ8837] SOLVEIG: There is only what is true

[chan#SQ8837] SOLVEIG: and what is not.

[chan#SQ8837] SOLVEIG: But no true thing is truer than another.

[chan#SQ8837] SOLVEIG: It's what makes truth vulgar.

[chan#SQ8837] SOLVEIG: The absence of discernment

[chan#SQ8837] SOLVEIG: and values.

[chan#SQ8837] SOLVEIG: Truth is pointless and dangerous.

[chan#SQ8837] SOLVEIG: It makes me puke.

[chan#SQ8837] LASZLO: That's a theoretical point of view.

[chan#SQ8837] LASZLO: Even you

[chan#SQ8837] LASZLO: can be angry or disappointed by someone who has lied to you.

[chan#SQ8837] LASZLO: Can't you?

[chan#SQ8837] SOLVEIG: Everyone lies.

[chan#SQ8837] SOLVEIG: Constantly.

[chan#SQ8837] SOLVEIG: And me too. I lie to everyone.

[chan#SQ8837] SOLVEIG: Including to myself.

[chan#SQ8837] SOLVEIG: So why would I be mad?

[chan#SQ8837] SOLVEIG: Or disappointed?

[chan#SQ8837] SOLVEIG: The lie changes nothing.

[chan#SQ8837] LASZLO: Changes nothing about what?

[chan#SQ8837] SOLVEIG: Any of it.

[chan#SQ8837] SOLVEIG: The fact that we are here,

[chan#SQ8837] SOLVEIG: to work,

[chan#SQ8837] SOLVEIG: to crawl painfully to the next day.

[chan#SQ8837] SOLVEIG: What other truth is there?

[chan#SQ8837] SOLVEIG: That I am lied to,

[chan#SQ8837] SOLVEIG: that I am told that I have always been lied to,

[chan#SQ8837] SOLVEIG: that an ultimate truth is revealed to me,

[chan#SQ8837] SOLVEIG: what would that change?

[chan#SQ8837] SOLVEIG: I will still get up in the morning.

[chan#SQ8837] SOLVEIG: I will still work.

[chan#SQ8837] SOLVEIG: I will die on the same day

[chan#SQ8837] SOLVEIG: at the same time

[chan#SQ8837] SOLVEIG: without anything changing.

[chan#SQ8837] SOLVEIG: The only truth is that we live here.

[chan#SQ8837] SOLVEIG: It's our job.

[chan#SQ8837] SOLVEIG: And that truth is immutable

[chan#SQ8837] SOLVEIG: because it is necessary.

[chan#SQ8837] SOLVEIG: Nothing will change it

[chan#SQ8837] SOLVEIG: because no one wants it to change.

[chan#SQ8837] LASZLO: What you are saying is that lies no longer exist.

[chan#SQ8837] LASZLO: That we already know everything there is to know.

[chan#SQ8837] LASZLO: And that, as a result, we can no longer lie?

[chan#SQ8837] LASZLO: Or be deceived?

[chan#SQ8837] SOLVEIG: No.

[chan#SQ8837] SOLVEIG: Lies exist.

[chan#SQ8837] SOLVEIG: Of course.

[chan#SQ8837] SOLVEIG: You can ask me what they will serve tomorrow in the cafeteria,

[chan#SQ8837] SOLVEIG: and I can answer that we will have venison stew,

[chan#SQ8837] SOLVEIG: when it's not true.

[chan#SQ8837] SOLVEIG: It will be a lie.

[chan#SQ8837] SOLVEIG: But under no circumstances will this lie have the power of any of the truths of this world.

[chan#SQ8837] SOLVEIG: What I'm saying isn't that lies don't exist,

[chan#SQ8837] SOLVEIG: it's just that there is no point to them.

[chan#SQ8837] SOLVEIG: And that the greatest of all lies

[chan#SQ8837] SOLVEIG: can never compete with the smallest of truths.

[chan#SQ8837] SOLVEIG: The lie is washed up.

[chan#SQ8837] SOLVEIG: It is dying.

[chan#SQ8837] SOLVEIG: It is a wounded fighter on the battlefield that other combatants step over without seeing.

[chan#SQ8837] SOLVEIG: The lie is a sideshow.

[chan#SQ8837] SOLVEIG: It is no longer the opposite of the truth.

# 7.
# OUR TRUST

Of all the known liars in the office, Théodore is by far the biggest.

Théodore is constantly at a thirty-degree angle, either in permanent acceleration when he walks, or perpetually swaying when he stands upright on the spot.

Looking at Théodore, anybody could understand many of the physical laws that govern our world – for example, gravity (if Théodore doesn't run, he falls; if Théodore runs, he falls) or centrifugal force (if Théodore doesn't turn, he falls; if Théodore turns, he falls) – because Théodore is a physical demonstration, a textbook case, whose personal trajectory traces a curve so regular around the temporal border of our reality that it appears deliciously spiroid.

However, while Théodore is physically irreproachable and regular, compensating perfectly on the one hand for what the physical laws have taken from him on the other, no one believes his stories anymore.

Because Théodore lies. Not satisfied with just lying, he doesn't hide it, claims responsibility for it and takes ownership of it.

Lying, for Théodore, is not depraved or vicious. His lies are innocent, transparent as glass, lies shaped like a heart that carries within it an apology.

Théodore does not lie just to lie, but to obey his calendar, which he is convinced will guide his friends and himself to an even better world than this one, already ideal.

Whether it exists or not, this calendar has never put us in harm's way, but we worry about the moment it will. On account of the lies and uncoordinated strategies, the ruses and misfires, it was obvious that one of our plans would fail, we would be delivered to the blades of the enemy, with no hope of survival, betrayed by this ridiculous accumulation of dates with no rhyme or reason.

A long time ago, we harassed him, interrogated him, resorted to blackmail to make him show us this object or admit that it was merely the ramblings of his offbeat brain. But Théodore never cracked. As absurd as it may seem, it was his calendar that had told him not to reveal to his colleagues whether or not it existed.

So, Théodore operated in the guild as a free electron. Generally, he followed the instructions of the group to the letter. But sometimes he disappeared in the middle of a raid to perform inane tasks set out in his stupid calendar. Similarly, we quickly understood that Théodore's word was not his bond. His actions and his words were dictated by his all-powerful calendar. We were tired of trying to distinguish truth from lies.

The decision to post him in front of Hick's cubicle during our conversation was therefore a decision by default. As the last member to join the guild, Théodore had statistically less chance of being recognized. His fairly reserved behaviour since he had come through the 8-Char Door guaranteed us relative anonymity, even though we ran the risk of him leaving his post to obey an impromptu order from his calendar.

This didn't seem to be the case. As we left Hick's cubicle, shortly before work resumed at 11:30, we found him in the corridor, in the same unstable position as we left him, and nothing suggested that he had taken off in the interval.

It was only in the afternoon, when enough time had passed for us to be convinced that our operation was successful, that Théodore wrote us on the guild's private network.

[chan#9926] THÉODORE: I forgot to tell you.

[chan#9926] THÉODORE: Something happened in front of the door [chan#9926] THÉODORE: while you were with Hick.

[chan#9926] THÉODORE: Well, it's a minor detail.

While we trust Théodore, it's a bloodless trust, with no flesh, a volatile and necessary membrane that separates us from the desire to kill him, but it is so thin that we can always make out on the other side the bloody murder that he has often deserved.

Our trust in Théodore is therefore not trust, or it is maybe its cousin, the genetic roots of which intersect with those of faith and a wilful blindness that no one dares call friendship.

# 8.
## A MINOR DETAIL

Just like the molecule of theine helps us open our eyes in the morning, collections of details help us stay alive every moment.

We smother ourselves in details, additional information, and encyclopedic clarifications. They are our fuel, our protectors, and our allies, to the point that missing a single one puts us in danger – and can be fatal.

Seemingly clear, the organization of our world can be broken down into millions of invisible laws that study and experience reveal one by one. So we plunge wholeheartedly into the abundant data. This constant stream of fragments of truth both reassures us and drives us to despair. While we know we are on the right track, the track of improvement, we also understand, given the infinite mass of existing knowledge, that we may never be able to grasp the totality.

After returning from Hick's cubicle, as this conversation starts, we are all tapping away while monitoring the data that flutters before our eyes. These are details of the world, the alphanumeric messengers each carrying a fraction of truth, themselves lies, but containing the statistical possibility that, one day, someone or something will bring them together, and that once this whole is understood and assimilated, the pure and ultimate truth will appear. This is the assumption that makes us love details, while we are appalled by their sad incompleteness.

[chan#9926] HICK: You like details?

Hick now has access to our private channel. In other words, he is part of our guild, although maybe he is not aware of it himself.

[chan#9926] CLARA: You'll see that we don't like details.

[chan#9926] CLARA: We need them.

[chan#9926] CLARA: This world is nothing more than a sum of details,

[chan#9926] CLARA: and all these details are available on our workstations,

[chan#9926] CLARA: at any moment.

[chan#9926] CLARA: It's what we see all day,

[chan#9926] CLARA: it's what we study.

[chan#9926] CLARA: The more we understand the details,

[chan#9926] CLARA: the more we understand the world

[chan#9926] CLARA: and the better we can brave it.

[chan#9926] HICK: Sorry, I understand, but

[chan#9926] HICK: focusing on details

[chan#9926] HICK: also cuts you off from a global vision of things.

[chan#9926] HICK: When it comes to thinking, it's the synthesis,

[chan#9926] HICK: the global vision, that's most important.

[chan#9926] HICK: Isn't it?

[chan#9926] HICK: By constantly massaging the millions of tiny components of a particular problem,

[chan#9926] HICK: by concentrating on a multitude of details and not on the whole,

[chan#9926] HICK: we run the risk of spending our lives drawing the wrong conclusions and maybe even committing absurd acts.

[chan#9926] SOLVEIG: The truth is pure only if it is complete.

[chan#9926] SOLVEIG: Your instructor didn't teach you that,

[chan#9926] SOLVEIG: in all those years?

[chan#9926] LASZLO: Calm down, Solveig.

[chan#9926] LASZLO: We're talking about truth and lies.

[chan#9926] LASZLO: Without all the data of a problem, Hick, the synthesis can only be a lie.

[chan#9926] LASZLO: No agent here has the mental faculties to understand the whole of everything we see each day.

[chan#9926] CLARA: Only the machines can.

[chan#9926] LASZLO: That's why we trust them to make every decision of our lives.

[chan#9926] SOLVEIG: Trying to synthesize is a risk no agent can afford.

[chan#9926] SOLVEIG: Because that synthesis will necessarily include an oversight.

[chan#9926] SOLVEIG: Because a decision made that way won't be a decision.

[chan#9926] SOLVEIG: It will be a mistake.

[chan#9926] SOLVEIG: On a large scale, that mistake will be called an ideology.

[chan#9926] SOLVEIG: You will learn that ideology is the worst thing there is.

[chan#9926] SOLVEIG: If you want to spend your life chasing an erroneous synthesis of the world,

[chan#9926] SOLVEIG: you will be an ideologue.

[chan#9926] SOLVEIG: And you won't last three days in this office.

[chan#9926] THÉODORE: Do you want to hear my story or not?

[chan#9926] LASZLO: Of course.

[chan#9926] THÉODORE: Here it is then.

[chan#9926] HICK: When I was at the institute, machines didn't help me make decisions.

[chan#9926] THÉODORE: Can I speak or not?

[chan#9926] HICK: Details were useless to me.

[chan#9926] HICK: I had to embrace the global vision of things.

[chan#9926] THÉODORE: Hello?

[chan#9926] CLARA: I don't think your attitude at the institute is a good example.

[chan#9926] CLARA: You were stuck there longer than any other agent before you.

[chan#9926] HICK: I didn't do what was expected of me.

[chan#9926] HICK: I used my head.

[chan#9926] HICK: Not machines.

[[chan#9926] HICK: And I'm still here.

[chan#9926] THÉODORE: Can I go now?

[chan#9926] LASZLO: Go ahead, Théodore. Tell us your story.

[chan#9926] THÉODORE: Thank you.

[chan#9926] THÉODORE: So, I was saying.

[chan#9926] CLARA: Keep it short.

[chan#9926] THÉODORE: You went into the cubicle and closed the door.

[chan#9926] SOLVEIG: Ah yes, I remember, it was fifteen minutes ago...

[chan#9926] LASZLO: Let him talk.

[chan#9926] THÉODORE: I don't know how many minutes had gone by, but I was waiting quietly, looking around me and over the cubicles, to check that I wasn't being recorded by a camera.

[chan#9926] THÉODORE: Anyway, I had my head down, and I was watching by lifting my eyes.

[chan#9926] THÉODORE: I don't know if you can picture it.

[chan#9926] THÉODORE: I'll show you at the break.

[chan#9926] CLARA: No, it's okay. We get it.

[chan#9926] CLARA: Go on.

[chan#9926] THÉODORE: Yeah, so, I was there, and I was waiting.

[chan#9926] SOLVEIG: And we came out.

[chan#9926] THÉODORE: No!

[chan#9926] THÉODORE: Let me finish, geez!

[chan#9926] LASZLO: Go on, go on.

[[chan#9926] THÉODORE: So, then someone approached me.

[chan#9926] THÉODORE: I heard him come up from behind.

[chan#9926] THÉODORE: I didn't know the guy, but he seemed to know this part of the floor.

[chan#9926] THÉODORE: He wasn't afraid.

[chan#9926] THÉODORE: He had his hands in his pockets, and he was whistling.

[chan#9926] THÉODORE: I was ready.

[chan#9926] THÉODORE: I had a letter opener in my pocket, and I was clutching it, even though I was telling myself that attacks never happen like this.

[chan#9926] THÉODORE: In fact, it seemed like a diversion,

[chan#9926] THÉODORE: so on top of watching the guy who was approaching, I was listening for what was happening around me,

[chan#9926] THÉODORE: in the cubicles and in the corridors.

[chan#9926] THÉODORE: Often, a guy is sent to make some noise near a target, and then the other assailants can sneak up and jump him.

No one says anything on the guild's encrypted channel. Because even though we have serious doubts about the truth of what Théodore is saying, there remains a non-zero chance that it is true. And if this is the case, the encounter is not a minor detail, if there is such a thing as a minor detail.

[chan#9926] THÉODORE: No sounds around me.

[chan#9926] THÉODORE: Just the murmur of Hick talking to you behind the partition.

[chan#9926] THÉODORE: By the way, Hick, you talk too loud.

[chan#9926] THÉODORE: You'll have to learn to keep your voice down.

[chan#9926] LASZLO: Go on.

[chan#9926] THÉODORE: So the guy approaches,

[chan#9926] THÉODORE: he looks at me,

[chan#9926] THÉODORE: he looks at Hick's cubicle,

[chan#9926] THÉODORE: then he says to me: 'Do you have the time?'

[chan#9926] HICK: Oof!

[chan#9926] HICK: I thought he was coming after me.

We are not as reassured as Hick. None of it makes sense. No one ever asks for the time in the office, nor probably in any other office. Why ask for the time? Everyone knows what time it is. When we are in front of our screens, it is permanently displayed, and when we are on break, we know exactly, viscerally, how many minutes remain before we have to go back to work. So, why ask the time? If not to provoke?

[chan#9926] THÉODORE: You can imagine my surprise.
[chan#9926] THÉODORE: He's testing me, I was thinking.
[chan#9926] THÉODORE: I decided to respond with the same tone.
[chan#9926] THÉODORE: I told him what time it was.
[chan#9926] SOLVEIG: What time was it?

With this uncharacteristically non-sarcastic intervention, Solveig is trying to figure out whether this event coincided with her vision of the regurgitated molecule in Hick's cubicle. More pragmatically, Théodore's answer would allow us to collect enough data to establish whether or not this story is true.

[chan#9926] THÉODORE: It was 11:19.
[chan#9926] LASZLO: And then?
[chan#9926] THÉODORE: Then I thought he would leave,
[chan#9926] THÉODORE: or that I would be attacked,
[chan#9926] THÉODORE: something like that.
[chan#9926] THÉODORE: But he said thank you and stood there,
[chan#9926] THÉODORE: smiling, looking at Hick's cubicle door from time to time.
[chan#9926] THÉODORE: After a few seconds, he said:
[chan#9926] THÉODORE: 'Is that the new guy's cubicle?'
[chan#9926] THÉODORE: So, I realized he wasn't going anywhere right away.
[chan#9926] THÉODORE: I didn't get flustered
[chan#9926] THÉODORE: and I did like we said.
[chan#9926] THÉODORE: I followed the plan.
[chan#9926] THÉODORE: I said: 'He's not a new guy now.'
[chan#9926] THÉODORE: That unnerved him, I think.
[chan#9926] THÉODORE: Because he thought before he went on.

[chan#9926] THÉODORE: And while he was thinking,

[chan#9926] THÉODORE: he took one step back,

[chan#9926] THÉODORE: and we all know what that means.

[chan#9926] HICK: What does it mean?

[chan#9926] CLARA: You need to learn body language.

[chan#9926] CLARA: They don't teach it at the institute, but it's vital.

[chan#9926] CLARA: I'll send you pages that talk about it on the global network.

[chan#9926] THÉODORE: And he just said: 'Ah.'

[chan#9926] THÉODORE: Then I heard fabric rustling behind me,

[chan#9926] THÉODORE: the type of rustling you do with your clothes when you want someone to hear you.

[chan#9926] THÉODORE: Apparently, they wanted me to know that the guy who was talking to me hadn't come alone.

[chan#9926] THÉODORE: I didn't need to think for very long.

[chan#9926] THÉODORE: They wanted a name.

[chan#9926] THÉODORE: They wanted to know what guild they were dealing with

[chan#9926] THÉODORE: and start the power games.

[chan#9926] THÉODORE: So, I did like we said.

[chan#9926] THÉODORE: I said:

[chan#9926] THÉODORE: 'In your opinion, in an aisle that turns red every night, do you think you're alone for long?'

[chan#9926] THÉODORE: And then he took another step back

[chan#9926] THÉODORE: and he relaxed a little.

[chan#9926] THÉODORE: I could see from his gestures and his face that he was giving up.

[chan#9926] THÉODORE: He understood what I was saying,

[chan#9926] THÉODORE: his friends too.

[chan#9926] THÉODORE: None of them wanted to rub the SB the wrong way.

[chan#9926] SOLVEIG: Hick, SB is the Scarlet Brigade.

[chan#9926] THÉODORE: He said: 'Ah yes, of course.'

[chan#9926] THÉODORE: Then: 'Goodbye, and thanks for the time.'

[chan#9926] THÉODORE: And he backed away and disappeared down a corridor.

[chan#9926] THÉODORE: There you have it.

We sat there a few seconds not writing anything. We didn't know what to make of the story, particularly how much credence to lend it. If it didn't happen, we had to understand for what twisted reason Théodore had invented it. And if it really happened the way Théodore told it, we had to take into account in our future actions the fact that at least one guild believed that Théodore was a Brigadier.

We didn't write anything more that afternoon, because, of the two theories, we were utterly incapable of saying which was the most dangerous for us. In either case, the story was clearly not a detail.

## PERSONALIZED NEWS

Thank you for consulting the news during your final break of the day.

Your productivity today was remarkable and remarked upon. Once again, the company noted that you are an invaluable resource. Stay the course, do not flag, and there will be a reward at the end of the road. Of course, keep this message strictly to yourself to avoid stirring up tensions and jealousy.

To clarify, the company recommends that you give no credence to the disruptive elements that insinuate that agents are not promoted. It is true that no agent from your office (0 out of 352) has recently received a reward. Nevertheless, these rewards do indeed exist, and you are in an excellent position to make liars of these unproductive agitators. We therefore encourage your discretion: clearly the facts, and only the facts, speak for themselves.

Do not waver, keep up the pace. Keep working with the same dedication. Get noticed for your seriousness and self-sacrifice. These are the guidelines you should follow.

## GENERAL NEWS

The company recommends extreme caution to agents going to sector D1. The east window was broken during the accidental fall of the employee who occupied cubicle 67. Said agent, Clay, as the video provided by an anonymous agent shows, tripped on a crease in the carpet, lost his balance, and unfortunately went through the window, propelled by his momentum.

The existence of this video eliminates the need for an investigation, and the death of Agent Clay has been ruled accidental. There is therefore no point in continuing to send whistleblowing messages to your liaison address.

# 9.
# THE ENTRAILS OF THE
# MODERN WORLD

We slip down the aisles and corridors of the office. The cubicles stream by on either side. We branch off at certain intersections, which reveal other corridors, other aisles, until we come to a stop. We pivot left. We are facing a cubicle with bullet marks on the door that form a constellation. The resemblance is striking. You don't need to be a member of the Astros guild to recognize the thirteen stars of Scorpio. It was an incredible coincidence that a hail of bullets made the impressions here, at the very spot where another venomous animal ran rampant. We approach. The image grows blurry. The door opens. When the sharpness returns, we are in Clara's cubicle.

'You should lie on your back, like this.'

With his half-closed eyes and a blissful smile, it's clear that the young man is no longer aware of anything. Clara smiles too, but for another reason. She doesn't seem to see us.

Judging from the number of bloodstained compresses in the trash can, the operation has been going on for at least half an hour. Clara has achieved the sadomasochistic trance she was seeking, which she reaches only through direct incisions on young flesh, and her own. On her body, and on that of her companion under local anaesthetic, a few stripes, purple, red, underlined with thin trickles of black blood in the darkness of the cubicle.

The young man is naked, and she is admiring the brown scars that form lines across the skin of her consenting partner, sunken memories, visible ghosts of ecstatic gestures executed a few months ago, some of which degenerated into keloids or hypertrophy, unpredictable effects that are rewards for an aesthete of the flesh. Lacerations, gashes, growths, puffiness, welts, and benign infections cover the young man's body.

She contemplates the wounds, the ones from today, before they heal. Before the biological mechanism rebels and changes potential death into a convalescent life.

She grabs her syringe and fills it with anaesthetic liquid without even looking at it, concentrating on the wounds. Laszlo can be heard in voice-over.

'The wounds are the game today. Maybe even the only game Clara has ever wanted to play, without believing herself skilled enough to get the job done. Today, it's different. How many years has she been studying human anatomy, physiology, post-traumatic shock, reactions to the different products she injects? How many nights has she spent reading on the global network everything that machines know about the bodies of their creators, and how many more putting this knowledge into practice? How many incisions? How many injections and then incisions? Litres of lidocaine and scalpel blades used during the countless exercises that were essentially training for today's operation? Just with this young man, who is not putting himself in her hands for the first time, who is resting still on his back as she slashes his flesh, how many? "Do what you want with me," was all he said at the beginning of the first session. That's what she did. Much more than to any of her other guinea pigs, and much more than to herself. Many of her interventions required a partner. She chose them from among the loners, the exhausted Underlins, the silent, about whom she wanted to know nothing, especially not their names. She saw them as a piece of her, like an extra limb, and vicariously experienced the pain and ecstasy of the bruising of the flesh.'

She cocks her head to admire the young man's lacerated body for a few more seconds.

This anonymous half-child, devoid of hope, envy, a future, and self-respect, silent or almost, is her greatest source of pride. Her favourite model, the one who will become the ultimate object of her fascination.

'Who's he?' the young man asks, stammering.

Clara makes a nonchalant gesture in the direction of the lens and Laszlo behind it.

'Oh, him… He's just my assistant. He's going to film us. I told you earlier.'

'Ah,' answers the young man, whose gaze ends up getting lost in the vision of a dark world from which he is absent, and it is more beautiful that way.

'So, this is it?' Laszlo asks, taking a step closer, so as not to miss any of Clara's whispered words.

'It's an incision I made a while ago.' She starts from under the lower right rib to reach its opposite point, going along the stomach, without touching the abdominal muscles. 'It's a sort of a smile. Like staking a claim. A warning to the flesh, letting it know I would be back.'

She inserts the syringe in two places, at either end of the young man's old scar on his belly, then a third time just above his navel, and, without waiting, prepares her scalpel.

'We didn't name this procedure,' Laszlo says. 'It is impossible for us to name a mystery. Here, everything will be new, surprising, everything will be novel. What we are going to see in a few seconds is less important than what we are going to feel. The title of this film will come to us only at the end of the shoot, when we will be gorged on emotion, and the reason for this act will emerge from this emotion.'

Laszlo zooms in on Clara's hand, and the lens caresses her scarified forearm, then slowly moves up toward her bare shoulder.

'Don't film my face.'

'Okay,' Laszlo answers, and pretends to abruptly change the frame, knowing full well he has already filmed Clara's face several times since he has been there.

'Now I'm going to make the incision,' Clara says. 'Don't move. And don't look. Or, if you look, imagine it's someone else's body, not yours. Someone you love, if you are capable of love. Someone who isn't here, but who you can see. Someone you know is suffering and that death for them will not be an ordeal but much anticipated relief.'

Clara waits for the young man's answer, but it doesn't come. She figures that the nameless agent has decided to think of himself, and that he recognizes himself in the description of the person who is suffering and who is no longer there. So, he is no longer there.

She gently presses her scalpel near the first injection point, at the very end of the scar, and slides the blade along the line already drawn on the young man's stomach. A trickle of blood escapes as the tool passes, and, like a book opening, a wave rising, the flesh spreads, allowing the bloody maelstrom to appear from the inside.

Laszlo makes no further comment. He is not trembling either. He applies himself to capturing every scene of the thrilling show he is witnessing: the gradual opening of the wound, the shiver through the muscles of the body, the ghostly immobility of Clara's fingers.

Around them, agents are sleeping, dreaming, calm or agitated. None of them are experiencing what they are, an experience both wild and precise, an emotional dive to the very heart of intimacy, to discover the perfect organization of this body that also makes them up.

Colours, shapes, combined, vibrant, organs, vessels, factories, transportation hubs, the functional network of life that runs through unaware workers and brings them alive, enzymes, globules, proteins, harnessed to their sole task, links in a closed chain, necessary to the whole, and the whole of which has no other goal than to serve its constituents, fractal image, stable galaxy held by the logical and immutable laws of biology, just like the invisible stars behind the grey sky held by the just as logical and immutable laws of physics.

'It doesn't look like what I have seen onscreen. It's a mess of blood and tissue. It's not organized. It's a heap. And that's what makes us walk and think. We are full of these viscous things. Our skin is a smooth sac that transports and hides this repulsive organism. We are sacs, envelopes that hide from others these disgusting messages and messages of disgust.'

'No, Clara,' Laszlo interrupts her. 'This is perfection in a system, and since our minds are imperfect, all we can see is the blood and quivering masses rubbing against each other. But perfection lives in the centre of this gaping wound. Look at how it moves and breathes. The stomach open, full of this repulsive filth, it lives. And we also live, we who are filled with this filth. We live, and the system lives, despite the disgust we have for it. What we are looking at, Clara, is a system. What we see quiver and ooze, you aren't dreaming, are the entrails of the modern world. Viscous, disgusting, incomprehensible, but perfect.'

'You've found a title for your film. And I'm going to sew him up.'

# 10.
## WHERE THE AIR IS LIQUID

The end of the month is approaching and with it the threat of unrest. Hick isn't the only one in danger. Dozens of Underlins with cubicles in ideal locations will soon suffer assaults from guilds seeking purchasing power. Members of historic guilds are also in the hot seat if their cubicles are strategically located. The computers have had time to reach their conclusions, and a number of scenarios now justify one guild attacking another, powerful though that guild may be. Strategists have even identified a scenario that compels an attack – there is so much to gain: it's the pincer position, where a cubicle is surrounded by three cubicles that belong to a single guild. The three cubicles cannot take out a Solidarity Loan since they aren't adjacent, so, if the agent caught in the pincer connects them, putting the four cubicles together multiplies their borrowing power. Agents who know they are caught in a pincer, regardless of the guild to which they belong, have no doubt that an attack is imminent, increasingly inevitable as the days go by. Attacks will be launched any moment, during any break, day or night, without warning. Including in the cafeteria.

It's the 14:30 break.

Standing single file in several rows, we are waiting our turn at the vending machines.

We do not stand side by side, for our safety, just like every time our guild shows itself in public. It's one of the implicit rules of the office: never reveal which guild you belong to, or even whether you belong to a guild.

Of all sources of protection, anonymity is by far the best, because a potential attacker will not attack when in doubt.

Statistics are an agent's allies. They don't lie. Anyone who challenges them leaves themselves open to violent reprisals. Offering information about ourselves means revealing one of the unknowns in the equation 'when to take us out' and, as a result, coming closer to the moment of its solution.

Solveig is pale. She advances, head down, like the others. The agents listen to identify the slightest sound that could signal danger, but Solveig seems to be somewhere else, tormented by a droning fear, which prevents her from hearing, seeing, or feeling.

Of all of us, she is the best positioned in the lines. She will be served first, and we fear this moment. That is why we are here – even Hick. If something happens, we aren't likely to intervene, for fear of giving away our affiliation. But sometimes just being there is enough.

The silence is thick, like it always is in the office, particularly during lunch hour. The agents drag their feet. One of them takes their plate and carries it toward their cubicle without looking up. Hick closes his eyes and finds himself imagining he is alone. No sounds, no words, just the distant flapping of the clothing of an employee falling from a higher floor. And the buzzer of the vending machine sounding at regular intervals announcing that a meal is ready.

'Excuse me, do you have the time, please?'

There must be around sixty agents here, in the cafeteria lineups. Everyone suddenly stops breathing as the sentence is uttered, incongruous and absurd, in this moment, in this place, not that it would have made sense anywhere else in the office.

We collect ourselves and look discreetly in the presumed direction of the agent who just spoke. What we see is as incongruous and senseless as what he said.

Théodore is fifth or sixth in line for the vending machine, swaying, and unlike the other agents who are waiting, he isn't looking down. His eyes are glued to the lineup beside him.

He watches a short, fat man, who is watching him back, eyebrows raised.

A few more seconds elapse. Théodore seems to be fighting with a bunch of contradictory ideas, none of which is the right one. Then he answers.

'It must be around 14:38.'

'Thanks a lot,' the short man answers, dropping his eyes and looking away from Théodore.

Throughout the lineups, the tension is palpable. No one understands what just happened. Hick, who until then thought he had heard the greatest silence possible, notices that now he is plunged into an even more complete void, to the point that the surrounding air has become liquid, almost thick, and that it is difficult to move, even to breathe. Everything has frozen in generalized slow motion. The fluidity of the world has been replaced by a series of fixed images, like immobile prisons, such that when the time comes to advance in the traumatized lineup's movement, an eternity seems to pass between the moment our brain sends the order to move the foot and the moment the foot advances.

Laszlo returns his attention to Solveig. He tells himself there will be plenty of time later to analyze what just happened. In a few seconds, she will be in front of the vending machine.

Four places behind him, Clara covertly observes the gestures and manners of the agents in line, taking fewer precautions than the others. Her face is so scarred and disfigured by successive operations that it has become a mask, with no muscles left to activate a recognizable sign of emotion, grimacing smiles, wooden pouts expressing the opposite of what they show. Clara notices, not far from Théodore, the young man whose innards she exposed last night. Since he seems to be doing okay, she smiles, even though the skin that slides along the bones of her skull does not evoke the image of a smile to anyone.

The agent in front of Solveig grabs his meal and disappears down the corridor. We hold our breath, while Solveig lifts her head and takes a step toward the machine's control panel. Laszlo squeezes his fists, as if he has forgotten that, no matter what happens, he cannot intervene. Clara relaxes all the muscles of her body, and her face falls like a piece of melted plastic. Théodore can't contain the flood of emotions overwhelming him. Frightened by the voiceless presence of the short, fat man, fearing a possible reaction from Solveig, rendered powerless by the surrounding air that is now liquid and paralyzing, as if the entire office is drowning in Clara's lidocaine, he is swaying more and more, without realizing it, obeying the physics of unfeasible balance, releasing outwardly the energy from inside.

Solveig consults the control panel with a weary look and already feels, at the mere sight of the dishes on offer, bile rise in her throat.

She is no longer here. She no longer sees us. She is no longer in the present. She is later, or earlier, on her hands and knees on the floor of a cubicle she doesn't recognize, surrounded by unknown, worried faces. She looks down and, through the tears distorting her vision, notices a pool, and in the middle of that pool, a tiny molecule of theine struggling to float, a molecule that does not have much longer to live, is on the verge of drowning, that is also breathing liquid, like everything in this office right now, like Laszlo who behind her resists the desire to help her, like the replacement Hick who is discovering the sort of tense situations agents face and who would like time to speed up, to no longer be here, to be far away, or before, perhaps even safe at the institute, alone with his instructor, alone but safe, and not in a lineup of enemies, accompanied by allies who would be no help to him anyway should something occur. And Solveig starts to tremble with the distress of her imaginary drowned molecule, reaches her hands toward the ground to save it, feeling the need to come to the rescue for the first time in her exist- ence, aware that this molecule was inside her, and that it was already drowning inside her, and that so many other things inside her are drowning and breathing liquid, in her stomach, prisoners of her and the flaccid mechanics of her entrails; then she opens her eyes and, with a horrible sound, vomits the contents of her empty stomach on the cafeteria control panel.

Like all of us, Théodore starts, and loses control of his rotation. Propelled backward, his body collides with the agent behind him, who loses his balance in turn and collides with the next one, in an inevitable chain reaction, given the limited space that separates the agents in line. Two employees fall backward, and the third uses his hand to search for purchase that will prevent him from doing likewise but finds only the liquid air and the stomach of the young man behind him, whom he hits with involuntary force, a mechanical dispersal of the speed of Théodore's body. A terrible snap rings in the dumbstruck agents' ears, and the shirt of the agent who was hit is stained with a scarlet liquid, of which only Clara and Laszlo know the source. The face of the young man who, the night before, was subjected to Clara's phantasmic work, freezes when he understands that the terrible noise is coming from his own body. The poorly stitched incision that was keeping his stomach closed opens under the force of the impact, and the gaping wound spills between the buttons of his shirt, and with a viscous gurgle his entrails spew onto the grey carpet of the office. Then he collapses, surprised to feel himself dying, his mouth desperately trying to snatch air that has grown too thick to reach his lungs.

Near the vending machine, Solveig also collapses onto all fours, tears in her eyes. Flouting the office safety rules, Laszlo lunges toward her to help her stand back up.

He slips his hands under her armpits but abandons his gesture when he meets her terrified eyes.

She presses herself against him, puts her mouth to his ear, and whispers as quietly as she can: 'Laszlo, I don't know what this means, but I think I'm pregnant.'

# 11.
## AN AGENT NAMED JUBH

'I demand an investigation! I demand an investigation!'

While the lineups scatter and people flee to their cubicles, an agent is shouting and gesticulating around the gutted body. He is sporting a thin moustache. He is not old, but early pattern baldness has formed a white disc on top of his head. He is the one who was knocked off balance in the lineup and hit the young man whose viscera is sullying the collective carpet. He is the one who killed him. He is the one responsible for a death and for defacing company property. He is the one who will be fired soon.

In a few seconds, he finds himself alone with a body in front of the vending machines. We too have gone back to our cubicles and are watching the scene on the general video feed.

Above us, we hear the characteristic hiss of the acid gas coming out of the ceiling. Soon a mobile cloud will gather and fly to the cafeteria to attack the dead agent's body. It will decompose his flesh, organs, and bones into a fine dust that will be sucked up by the office's ventilation system.

'My name is Jubh, and I demand an investigation! Copiers, I need your services!'

On the video feed, we see the cloud hovering over the cafeteria. The agent named Jubh sees it too. In an act of desperation, he leans over the body, as if to intervene, all the while knowing, like all of us, that if the acid cloud descends on him, he will suffer the same fate as the body of our enemies fallen in combat, turned into agent powder, finally at peace.

[chan#9926] LASZLO: Is everyone okay?

[chan#9926] SOLVEIG: I'm okay.

[chan#9926] HICK: What just happened?

[chan#9926] THÉODORE: I'm dead.

[chan#9926] LASZLO: Clara?

[chan#9926] CLARA: I'm okay.

The acid cloud slows. Agent Jubh freezes, palm open, as if he were trying to subdue a wild animal from the before times, as if the cloud has a will of its own and isn't controlled by an office cleaning program, as if the gas has eyes to see and ears to hear. But the cloud stops, and an agent enters from the right corner of the image. He approaches Agent Jubh and holds out a hand.

[chan#9926] THÉODORE: It's the Brigadiers.

[chan#9926] THÉODORE: The short, fat guy is a Brigadier, and he
    knows I pretended to be one of them.

[chan#9926] THÉODORE: They're going to kill me.

[chan#9926] HICK: Can someone tell me what's going on?

[chan#9926] LASZLO: Not now, Hick.

SPECIAL MESSAGE – INVESTIGATION UNDER WAY
Following the events that occurred today at 14:39 in the cafeteria on the 122nd floor, the company would like to inform you that it has opened investigation MD66373 to determine the causes of the incident that led to the death of an agent and the defacement of company property. Agent Jubh, the main suspect in this incident, has hired the Copiers guild to defend him and conduct a counter-investigation. While this procedure is ongoing, the agents from that floor (122) are asked to co-operate with investigators and not impede the investigation in any way whatsoever.

Behind the company messages and the discussions on our private channel, the video window keeps showing the image of the cafeteria.

We can see the acid cloud stop its advance and dissolve in the air. The Copier photographs the scene from different angles. Other agents join him. They bring a large plastic tarp in which they roll the body, taking care to gather up his organs.

[chan#9926] CLARA: We have to do something.
[chan#9926] THÉODORE: The Brigadiers are going to take me out.
[chan#9926] CLARA: The Copiers are a force to be reckoned with.
[chan#9926] CLARA: They will clear Jubh and pin it on one of us.
[chan#9926] CLARA: On Solveig because she vomited.
[chan#9926] CLARA: On Théodore because he fell.
[chan#9926] THÉODORE: I'm dead.
[chan#9926] CLARA: Or on me.
[chan#9926] HICK: Why you?
[chan#9926] HICK: This has nothing to do with you.
[chan#9926] HICK: You were in another line.
[chan#9926] LASZLO: Not now, Hick.

While we are talking, our computers gobble up the information and chew on it, one piece at a time, adding each piece to the problem. But the algorithms are running in a loop. Assessing factors that would clear one of the members of our guild would lead necessarily to the indictment and fall of another.

[chan#9926] LASZLO: Our only hope is to invoke Fung's Law.

SPECIAL MESSAGE – INVESTIGATION UNDERWAY
As part of the defence of Agent Jubh following the incident of 14:39 that occurred today in the cafeteria, the Copiers guild has submitted two requests to the company.

The first is a request for authorization to perform an autopsy on the victim's body. This request has been granted provided the autopsy is performed in a public place equipped with a company surveillance camera to document the operation.

The second is a request to make available the videos from the cafeteria 30 minutes before and 30 minutes after the incident. This request has been accepted and the videos deposited in the file.

[chan#9926] CLARA: Fung's Law is difficult to argue.

[chan#9926] LASZLO: But you know what the autopsy will show.

[chan#9926] HICK: What's Fung's Law?

[chan#9926] LASZLO: Later, Hick.

[chan#9926] LASZLO: The videos will show that a Brigadier spoke to Théodore.

[chan#9926] LASZLO: It made him lose his balance.

[chan#9926] THÉODORE: It's in my calendar.

[chan#9926] LASZLO: It's an additional cause of the incident.

[chan#9926] LASZLO: If they can show that all these factors are of equal importance,

[chan#9926] LASZLO: including what Jubh did –

[chan#9926] THÉODORE: I just noticed.

[chan#9926] LASZLO: – then the case will be decided.

[chan#9926] THÉODORE: It's now.

[chan#9926] HICK: Ah yes, I remember.

[chan#9926] HICK: Fung's Law on the convergence of factors.

[chan#9926] THÉODORE: I'm sorry, but my calendar says so.

[chan#9926] CLARA: What are you talking about?

[chan#9926] CLARA: What is your calendar saying?

[chan#9926] THÉODORE: It's over.

[chan#9926] THÉODORE: It's now.

We immediately understand the gravity of the situation. Théodore is cracking up. We sensed he was vulnerable, worried, but who isn't today? In a way, we were thinking that his gentle madness protected him from the shadows that often swaddle and rock us with morbid nursery rhymes. Long after us, he is finally realizing that the discussion he had in front of Hick's cubicle is no mere detail, that he is under threat, that that threat is not distant but will be acted on soon, maybe during the next break. Even his ridiculous calendar can no longer reassure him.

[chan#9926] LASZLO: Whatever you're planning to do, Théodore, don't do it.

[chan#9926] LASZLO: At least wait until the break.

[chan#9926] LASZLO: There are no times on your calendar. It can wait till the break.

[chan#9926] THÉODORE: Of course there are times,

[chan#9926] THÉODORE: what do you think?

It's 15:06.

The break is in two hours and thirty-nine minutes, and that deadline throws in our faces our responsibilities as imperfect humans. This is one of the rare cases when machines can't help; launching one of them to tell us the best plan to execute in two hours and thirty-nine minutes would be a waste of time: the analysis of variables would take more time than we have. The only rapid response the machine would give would be that an agent cannot obtain a response to this sort of request in such a short time.

[chan#9926] LASZLO: What is your calendar telling you, Théodore?

We are all waiting for a response from our colleague, some of us even forgetting to monitor the data intersecting over the dialogue, the messages from the company, the videos of the incident in the cafeteria, which the Copiers are playing in a loop.

[chan#9926] THÉODORE: It doesn't say anything more, Laszlo.

[chan#9926] THÉODORE: I just noticed.

[chan#9926] THÉODORE: It ends today.

[chan#9926] THÉODORE: Today is the last date.

[chan#9926] THÉODORE: After that, there's nothing.

[chan#9926] THÉODORE: They're going to attack.

[chan#9926] THÉODORE: The Brigadiers are going to take me out.

[chan#9926] THÉODORE: As soon as I stick my nose outside the
cubicle.

[chan#9926] THÉODORE: At 17:45,

[chan#9926] THÉODORE: or at 21:00.

[chan#9926] THÉODORE: But today.

[chan#9926] THÉODORE: It's inevitable.


   Some of us think that the invisible calendar never existed, that
it is a fantasy object that Théodore invented to manifest his fears
and keep them outside himself. Obeying one's madness and stupidity can be harrowing, and everyone finds strategies not to do it.
These methods take different forms, from total amnesia to inventing
things that don't exist, and so we concluded that Théodore attributed
to his calendar all the senseless choices for which he was unable to
assume responsibility.
   Nevertheless, at this very moment, whether Théodore's calendar
is real or not, the result is the same. Because, for our colleague, the
end of the calendar means the end of him.


[chan#9926] LASZLO: Maybe you'll find another calendar. Time doesn't
stop, Théodore.

[chan#9926] THÉODORE: You're kind,

[chan#9926] THÉODORE: but that's not true.

[chan#9926] THÉODORE: Universal time doesn't stop; that's true.

[chan#9926] THÉODORE: Agents are born

[chan#9926] THÉODORE: and die,

[chan#9926] THÉODORE: and are replaced by other agents.

[chan#9926] THÉODORE: That's the way it has always been

[chan#9926] THÉODORE: and always will be.

[chan#9926] THÉODORE: But the calendar is not the universal calendar.

[chan#9926] THÉODORE: It's mine

[chan#9926] THÉODORE: and it's reaching its end.

[chan#9926] THÉODORE: There is nothing more to say.

[chan#9926] THÉODORE: I'm sorry for all the trouble I'm causing you.

[chan#9926] THÉODORE: I hope the replacement who takes over my cubicle will be less batty than me.

[chan#9926] THÉODORE: And more efficient.

[chan#9926] THÉODORE: And that they will be more help to you.

[chan#9926] THÉODORE: But now, it's over.

[chan#9926] THÉODORE: I'm leaving you.

[chan#9926] THÉODORE: Thank you for having been such good colleagues.

[chan#9926] THÉODORE: I am proud to have worked alongside you.

[chan#9926] THÉODORE: Goodbye.

The guild's channel goes silent.

There are still two hours and thirty minutes before the break, long minutes during which we can only wait and keep working, without knowing whether Théodore is dead or dying.

No one says anything. There is nothing to say. It's a terrible moment. We jump in hope with each word that appears on the network, only to realize it's just another desperate call from Laszlo.

[chan#9926] LASZLO: Théodore?

[chan#9926] LASZLO: Théodore?

[chan#9926] LASZLO: Théodore?

[chan#9926] LASZLO: Théodore?

[chan#9926] LASZLO: Théodore?

[chan#9926] LASZLO: Théodore?

[chan#9926] LASZLO: Théodore?

[chan#9926] LASZLO: Théodore?

[chan#9926] LASZLO: Théodore?

[chan#9926] LASZLO: Théodore?

[chan#9926] LASZLO: Théodore?

[chan#9926] LASZLO: Théodore?

[chan#9926] LASZLO: Théodore?

[chan#9926] LASZLO: Théodore?

[chan#9926] LASZLO: Théodore?

[chan#9926] LASZLO: Théodore?
[chan#9926] LASZLO: Théodore?
[chan#9926] LASZLO: Théodore?
[chan#9926] LASZLO: Théodore?

This tragic column scrolls by in jerky slowness on our screens and traces our colleague's horrible digital tomb, the oldest line disappearing after a few seconds, the column growing that much shorter. We imagine Laszlo, unable to accept the idea that it will disappear completely, insisting on typing Théodore's name over and over, without waiting for a response, so that the column will not disappear, and with it the memory of someone who has been with us for so long.

# 12.
# BECOMING A GHOST

SPECIAL MESSAGE – INVESTIGATION UNDERWAY
As part of the defence of Agent Jubh in investigation MD66373, the Copiers guild has delivered its autopsy report. The report indicates that the victim's body showed evidence of surgery to the stomach and a large wound stitched with poor quality thread. The Copiers would like to submit to the file the following finding: 'The impact inflicted by Agent Jubh is not the cause of the victim's death. If he had not suffered this degradation of his physical integrity, the victim would have survived the collision. Furthermore, given the location and size of the wounds, the surgery could not have been performed by the victim himself.' The defence would therefore like the agent responsible for the operation on the victim to be identified and heard before possible indictment.

If you have information that will lead to locating this agent, the company strongly encourages you to make it public. Mutual assistance and solidarity are essential between employees, and the company reminds you that it is an agent's duty to help another agent, for the well-being of the group and the smooth operation of the office. A denunciation form can be found on the global network.

The second our clocks show 17:45, despite the dangers that weigh on our lives, we rush through the corridors and aisles toward Théodore's cubicle.

Laszlo arrives first, even though his cubicle is the furthest, and he pushes on the door, which visibly isn't locked.

When we join him, we find him bent over Théodore's body. He is wading in a puddle of fresh blood. At first we think he is holding his colleague in a final embrace.

Yet a curious, guttural sound can be heard, and when Laszlo turns back toward us, we see that he isn't holding him, but rather pressing his bloody hands on Théodore's neck.

'He's not dead,' he says. 'He must have missed the artery. He's lost blood, but we can save him.'

Théodore has never been a great killer, and fortunately this applies to his suicide attempt today. In the pool of blood, we can make out the letter opener he must have planted in his throat, hoping to sever one of his carotid arteries but hitting cartilage and his trachea.

Clara takes off running toward her cubicle.

'Let me die,' Théodore snarls, in a liquid, bubbling voice, a horrifying shift in sound that makes clear to those who haven't seen the injury the toll it is taking.

'You're not going to die,' Laszlo answers gently, as he continues to put pressure on the wound to stop the bleeding.

'I'm wounded,' Théodore says. 'I'm no longer any use to you. Let me die, then wait for my replacement. Anyhow, I'm doomed. The Brigadiers are going to come after me.'

'You're not doomed,' Clara responds, having already returned, holding in her scarified fingers bandages and suturing equipment.

Laszlo throws her a dirty look. If she were to have been caught in the corridors of the office with her instruments, she would have been denounced that very second.

Clara doesn't respond, approaches Théodore and grimaces, something we have never seen her do and that is impossible to interpret. We deduce that she is not smiling, that she is not angry, and that she is not afraid.

'Where's Solveig?' she asks.

'Solveig isn't coming,' Laszlo says in a monotone, as if the information were incidental. 'Tell us what we have to do. We have less than fifteen minutes to stabilize him.'

Without showing the slightest emotion, Clara pulls from her pockets a syringe and a vial of translucent liquid. Laszlo takes out his camera.

'Hick, you're going to hold him,' Clara says. 'Once I've injected this, he will sleep until the next break. We're going to stop the bleeding now, and later, when he wakes up, I'll have something to propose to him.'

Théodore doesn't react. He continues to moan, awaiting death, hoping it will be imminent so that no one has time to administer restorative care.

Laszlo films Clara. He nods in agreement, seeming to understand what she will propose.

'That's a good idea,' is all he says.

'What?' Hick asks. 'What's a good idea?'

'I'm going to make him a ghost,' she answers.

Théodore is in danger. That's a fact. It's why we didn't blame or ridicule him for what he did. In the same situation, what would we have done? Who would have had the courage to face the Scarlet Brigade rather than putting an end to it first? And yet the choice to save him isn't an obvious one, for any of us. Théodore is not reliable. Any replacement who arrived today to take his place would be a bigger help to us, despite their youth and inexperience. But Clara gets to work. And Laszlo approves. And Hick offers his assistance. And we do everything we can to save him. Are we cynical enough to try to protect one of our members by pretending to save another? Deep down, doesn't Clara think there is a tiny chance that Théodore will be held responsible for the incident in the cafeteria? With Théodore dead, the list of suspects shrinks and puts her directly at risk. Logically, keeping Théodore alive is a way to protect the guild in general and her in particular. Are we such monsters? Rattlesnakes ready to strike our own colleagues, our own allies?

For Théodore to no longer fear reprisals from the Scarlet Brigade, for him to survive long enough to remain a bulwark against the Copiers' investigation, Clara has a plan.

'The company is watching us, you know,' she says to him. 'There are cameras everywhere, invisible, in the recesses of this office, and those cameras identify us. To recognize us, the machines don't have the same points of reference as we do. They are more precise, more efficient, and rely on biometric control points that no agent can detect without a detailed, assisted study. You know the software. We use it without understanding how it works. It helps us spot an enemy in the corridors or extract the desired face from a crowd of employees. Few agents have studied the algorithms and learned the points of reference in their free time. But I have. That's why I've never had a problem with the company despite how I have disfigured my face and body. To anyone else, I don't look anything like the person who stepped through the 8-Char Door. But for the machines that are watching us, I haven't changed, because I have always been careful in my modifications to keep the exact measurements for biometric recognition of my original face. What I'm trying to tell you is that you can become someone else. I can change you so that no one who sees your face will see the man who impersonated a Brigadier in the corridors of the west gallery. Of course, the operation won't stand up to machine analysis, but who will ask for that analysis if you're not suspected with a first inquisitive look? I'm offering you a chance to disappear, Théodore. I'm offering you, while remaining with us, in this office, to escape the Scarlet Brigade. I am offering to make you a ghost.'

Théodore's face becomes more serious, less melodramatic. We realize that he wasn't suffering as much as he seemed to be and was overplaying his agony.

'I don't have a calendar anymore,' he finally says. 'How can I make a decision?'

'What if, for once, you tried thinking?' Hick asks.

# 13.
# THE SMOKERS

The surgery takes place in the middle of the night. The office is not asleep. The end of the month keeps the inciting attackers and the watchful defenders on alert. Clara handles her instruments with dexterity, while muffled noises resonate intermittently in different sectors. Sometimes cries rise above the hum of the ventilation. It's an Underlin who doesn't have the fortitude to die in silence. It's a pincer closing on the cubicle of a condemned agent. More rarely, gunfire is exchanged, a gunfight that lasts many long minutes. We assume a guild has found an adversary worthy of it. Then calm is restored. The geography of the 122nd floor mutates. The balance of power shifts. The system rights itself. Yet we know that a fire is smouldering, that there is a bomb threat. It's the Copiers' investigation that is preventing war from breaking out. The guilds are dusting off their weapons, honing their tactics, shaping their ambitions. When the time comes, tomorrow, in one month, in one year, conflict will be inevitable. Violent and bloody, it will redraw the physiognomy of the entire office. We doubt we will survive this Armageddon, and we try to stall for time, to at least have the leisure to witness it. We are convinced that there will be a sort of beauty nestled in the horrific folds of this massacre.

When she has finished with Théodore, Clara throws her equipment in the recycling airlock. If the investigation were to lead to her, it would be damning evidence, even more than her disfigured face, her lacerated body.

[chan#9926] CLARA: It's done.

[chan#9926] LASZLO: Théodore?

[chan#9926] LASZLO: Are you back in your cubicle?

[chan#9926] THÉODORE: My calendar has ended.

[chan#9926] THÉODORE: Why has it ended?

[chan#9926] THÉODORE: And yet I'm still here?

An explosion reverberates near sector Z. It's a few metres from Laszlo's cubicle. We reflect on the fact that no one is ever safe. Ever.

[chan#9926] LASZLO: We still have a problem to deal with.

[chan#9926] LASZLO: Hick.

[chan#9926] HICK: I'm a problem?

[chan#9926] CLARA: I have some useful information.

[chan#9926] LASZLO: Not now, Hick.

Even if Théodore is off the hook, Hick is still in danger. The Bookies and the guilds that overheard the conversation between Théodore and the short, fat man won't attack, believing that Hick's cubicle is under the control of the Scarlet Brigade. Even if, as we suspect, he is a Brigadier, the short, fat man will have understood that it is a cubicle to capture, that we are nothing, that they just have to dispose of the eccentric replacement and wait for the one who will take his place, with full pay and the promise of a greater borrowing limit.

[chan#9926] LASZLO: What information, Clara?

[chan#9926] CLARA: I spent weeks scouting

[chan#9926] CLARA: for my scarlet happening.

[chan#9926] CLARA: I slipped into the bathroom at night,

[chan#9926] CLARA: to take measurements.

[chan#9926] CLARA: And I noticed that once a week,

[chan#9926] CLARA: in the middle of the night,

[chan#9926] CLARA: agents gather there.

[chan#9926] CLARA: There are six of them. Always the same ones.

[chan#9926] CLARA: Always the same day of the week.

[chan#9926] CLARA: They stay there for around an hour, then leave,

[chan#9926] CLARA: and they all go their separate ways.

[chan#9926] LASZLO: Do you know what they're doing in there?

[chan#9926] CLARA: I had my suspicions.

[chan#9926] CLARA: Every time I went into the bathroom right after them,

[chan#9926] CLARA: there was a smell.

[chan#9926] LASZLO: The smell of tobacco.

[chan#9926] CLARA: Exactly.

[chan#9926] HICK: They were smoking in the bathroom?

[chan#9926] HICK: It's against the rules!

[chan#9926] LASZLO: How is this information useful to us?

[chan#9926] CLARA: Because I never saw any of the smokers again,

[chan#9926] CLARA: until I stumbled upon a familiar face

[chan#9926] CLARA: while watching the videos the Copiers are showing in a loop.

[chan#9926] CLARA: I'm sure of it. The man Théodore calls the short, fat man is one of them, one of the agents who smoke at night.

[chan#9926] CLARA: I hadn't seen his face in the cafeteria

[chan#9926] CLARA: when he asked Théodore for the time.

[chan#9926] CLARA: But now I'm sure.

[chan#9926] CLARA: It's him.

[chan#9926] CLARA: He's a smoker.

[chan#9926] LASZLO: The smokers are Brigadiers.

[chan#9926] CLARA: And tomorrow is the day they get together.

Our machines are humming again. The equation data merges, rotates, pivots. The streams of results are filtered. We need an action plan for this very night. Every hour wasted is an hour that Hick is in danger. Even though it will deprive us of sleep and hinder our productivity for tomorrow, the sacrifice is necessary. Better to be exhausted than dead. All night, we watch the machines that calculate and produce hypotheses. The numbers scroll by. The information intermingles. We have the unpleasant impression that we will never stop working.

Day breaks on more hours of weariness. The hot plates hum, the water boils, the molecules of theine spread in the water and sully the limpidity, like shame stains our clear consciences.

At five o'clock, the agents get down to work. All night, the emergency XO signal does not appear on our screens. We are thrilled to know Hick is safe and sound. He has to hold out five quarter-hours, five breaks during which he is at risk of an attack, before the night-time break, when we will put our plan into action.

SPECIAL MESSAGE – INVESTIGATION UNDERWAY

The company would like to remind all agents that it is their duty to report any criminal act. If you have knowledge of an agent who has information related to investigation MD66373 and who refuses to make it public, show bravery and report them to the company.

Similarly, if you know an agent who will not report an agent who refuses to make public information related to investigation MD66373, show courage and report them to the company. You can find on the global network the denunciation form, the failure to denounce reporting form, and, if needed, the reporting form for knowledge of failure to report failure to denunciate.

The day goes by without a hitch. At the 17:45 break, we start to think we just may make it. At the nine o'clock break, our hope grows even more.

[chan#9926] HICK: I'm hungry.

[chan#9926] CLARA: You'll eat tomorrow.

[chan#9926] HICK: You could have brought me something from the cafeteria.

[chan#9926] CLARA: You just got here and already you want to break a rule.

[chan#9926] HICK: Tea doesn't fill my stomach.

[chan#9926] LASZLO: Just three minutes until the break.

[chan#9926] LASZLO: Hick, be ready. I'll be there at 12:15.

[chan#9926] LASZLO: And I might not be the only one.

[chan#9926] LASZLO: Open your door only if I tap out the right code.

The clock on our screens reads 00:15, and a few seconds later, the first explosions ring out, muffled, solitary messengers of acts we imagine are meticulous and targeted. The latent war the office is teeming with will never end. It is like the sound of thunder during a summer storm, distant but all around us, permanent and invisible.

Laszlo creeps toward Hick's cubicle. To get there, he avoids the central aisle, takes a few detours, and hears the fanatical cries of the Brigadiers rising up with varying degrees of clarity from the cubicles along the west window. Night after night, they seem to be more numerous, crazier, more enraged. Once the sky starts to turn red, they shout more than sing hymns to the glory of the Brigade. They promise an impending revelation, a red paradise, bliss for all eternity working in the most beautiful spot in the office; they describe a fantastical future where the union of all Brigadiers from all floors of the tower will complete their twilight utopia. Just a few weeks ago, these songs stopped at sundown. Increasingly, they carry on into the night and grow in volume.

[chan#9926] HICK: Théodore, it's Laszlo.

[chan#9926] HICK: I'm in Hick's cubicle.

[chan#9926] HICK: Are you in place?

[chan#9926] THÉODORE: I'm ready.

[chan#9926] CLARA: Don't waste your energy.

[chan#9926] CLARA: The smokers come out a lot later.

[chan#9926] HICK: You never know.

[chan#9926] HICK: It's not a non-zero chance.

After a thunderous finale, a new song starts. But there aren't as many singers. It feels like some of the Brigadiers have broken ranks with the choir.

'Go on,' Laszlo says. 'They'll be done soon. Take the shortest route. Don't go too near the cubicles and don't stop for anything.'

'Wouldn't it be safer to stay here with you?' Hick asks. 'We'd be stronger together than apart, no?'

'The statistics of the plan say otherwise. If the Brigadiers attack this cubicle, it's better if I'm alone to defend it. If I die, my cubicle stays in our guild, and you keep yours. Temporarily. But if, on the other hand, you're killed, not only will we lose this cubicle, but the Scarlet Brigade grows exponentially stronger. You hear them when they're singing? They're surrounding us. Your cubicle could even be caught in a pincer.'

Hick looks incredulous.

'You'll get it eventually,' Laszlo says. 'You'll pick up this stuff fast. You don't have a choice. Go on, go.'

Hick decides not to ask another question, opens the door, and rushes out of the cubicle. Laszlo closes the door and listens. No gunshot, no fight, no groans, no sounds for a minute: Hick must be long gone. No one was targeting them.

He walks around the office and sits on the chair, facing the screen. Three hours later, he is in the same position when messages gleam on the private channel window.

[chan#9926] THÉODORE: There is movement.
[chan#9926] THÉODORE: An agent just went into the bathroom.
[chan#9926] THÉODORE: And another.

Théodore is holding above the partition wall a piece of mirror attached to a metal rod.

[chan#9926] HICK: We wait until all six of them go in.
[chan#9926] HICK: Hick, are you ready?

[chan#9926] LASZLO: I'm ready.

[chan#9926] LASZLO: Finally.

[chan#9926] LASZLO: Are you sure there's nothing to be afraid of?

[chan#9926] CLARA: In absolute terms, it's very risky.

[chan#9926] CLARA: But statistically it's less risky than going back to
your cubicle and doing nothing.

[chan#9926] LASZLO: Okay.


Théodore counts two more agents, then a minute later, two more. The smokers are all there. The green light is given. Hick adjusts his collar, tugs on the velvet of his pants, takes a deep breath, and exits Laszlo's cubicle. He heads down the corridor, not too fast, not too slow. He feels like his steps are making an ungodly racket on the carpet. While passing through sector T, he thinks he hears a whimper behind a door. It could be his own. In every cubicle, someone is dying or suffering; in that one, they're doing it noisily. He turns down the aisle that leads to the bathrooms. At the base of some of the partition walls, grids of red lights indicate the area is booby-trapped. Hick doesn't pay any attention to it; he stays in the middle of the aisle. We explained to him that agents' protective devices are often invisible. Motion detectors, heat sensors, weight sensors, devices much more discreet than crude laser systems. If he survives until the end of the month, he will get his half pay and maybe can buy one next year. Or he won't need it. The plan will have worked, and the Scarlet Brigade will keep its distance.

A series of weak explosions, like plastic bubbles bursting, make him jump. They are coming from the central aisle, somewhere on his right. He would like to speed up, but he is afraid that will make even more noise. Did a door just open in sector R? Is an eye watching him through the crack? Is a gun trained on him? Or is it his imagination producing sounds and images from the noises and shadows of the office at night?

Just ten more metres. He is not far from Solveig's cubicle but doesn't know it. The bathrooms are right there; he can see them.

Just a few more steps, and he will appear in Théodore's spy mirror. His mouth goes dry. He has a hard time swallowing. He feels like his legs don't have the strength to carry him. He has arrived in front of the door to the bathrooms. His hands are trembling, his shoulders are trembling. He hopes his voice won't tremble. He pulls Laszlo's camera from under his tunic and starts recording, points the lens straight ahead, and places his hand on the door handle.

[chan#9926] THÉODORE: Okay. He's going in.
[chan#9926] HICK: Everything's good on my end.
[chan#9926] HICK: Everything is being recorded.
[chan#9926] HICK: I'm launching the live feed.

At first the image is blurry and shadowy, but focusing reveals that it is not just the camera: a thick cloud of smoke has filled the room. The six Brigadiers are standing in the grey wreaths in front of us. Recognizable for his size, the short, fat man is indeed part of the group. Like the others, he is smiling. Their hands are empty. No cigarettes, no cigars, nothing smoking.

'You thought you would catch us that easily?' the short, fat man asks. 'You thought we didn't have detectors to alert us when an imbecile like you has an urgent need to attack the Scarlet Brigade in the middle of the night? You thought you could show up here with your camera and expose us?'

It is all Hick can do not to tremble, to put on a calm, undaunted face. 'No,' he answers. 'I'm here to tell you two things.'

The Brigadiers make a barely perceptible movement that, to an experienced agent, indicates surprise, concern.

'The first,' Hick says, 'is that thanks to the Q2 cameras we placed in the bathrooms on the 21:00 break' – he shows them the small black dots on the bathroom walls; they look like raisins, deposits of grime – 'we are recording everything that happens here. We saw you go in. We saw you light your cigarettes. We even saw you chuck them just before I came in. These videos belong to us. They are secure, safe on our encrypted servers.'

On the screen, the faces of the Brigadiers fall. They are stunned, stupefied. Hick goes on.

'The second thing is that if you try to take any action against me, directly or indirectly, we will make the videos public. You will gain one cubicle. You will lose six.'

Hick marks a pause. He presses the camera's rec button to stop the recording. The Brigadiers are frozen, their brains unable to calculate the stance they should take.

'Leave me alone,' Hick says. 'Leave me alone.'

And he backs up a step, closes the door, and lets the Scarlet Brigade ruminate for eight months.

Eight months of tension and extreme vigilance. Eight months like a long winter. Eight months filled with moments that could be the last.

## GENERAL NEWS

As we reminded you on the general news feed, Cily Vinière-Banks, new CEO of the west zone of Chicago 3, has committed to visiting the facilities under her responsibility one by one to gather comments or complaints from agents.

For agents in tower 35S, tomorrow will be the eagerly awaited day when Ms. Vinière-Banks's aircraft will touch down on the roof of your tower. She will meet your designated representative at 12:00.

For your representative to get the most out of the few minutes of conversation granted to them, we encourage you to send them now, if you have not already, your message for Ms. Vinière-Banks.

You will find the contact information for your representative on the global network, in the section dedicated to your tower. Be sure to consult the requests already made by your colleagues to avoid redundancy as much as possible.

## INVESTIGATION UNDERWAY

As part of the defence of Agent Jubh regarding investigation MD66373, the Copiers guild would like the following evidence to be placed in the file: video of the surgical intervention illegally conducted on the victim, by an agent soon to be identified.

The spokesperson for the Copiers adds that this new evidence irrefutably proves that the deadly surgery was what led to the death of the victim and not the minor mechanical action of their client, which any normally constituted agent would have survived. The Copiers now request a motion to dismiss for their client and the initiation of legal proceedings against the agent responsible for the fatal intervention. They remain available to the company if it would like to use their services to analyze the video and flush out the offender. Their estimate is attached to the communiqué.

# 14.

# BREASTS ON RIBS

This morning, the news feed is not merely giving us news. It is pointing to a moment to come, soon, when the time bomb patiently waiting under the floor of the office will explode. We are doomed. We know it.

The network is silent, stunned, and the announcement of the existence of the accusatory video is not being debated. What will debate change in the case? We knew this moment was coming. It's here.

So, it's the silence of work, our eyes and our minds trained on studying the data we are sent, applied, serious, the rest hidden inside us like the sun behind the clouds, powerful enough to change night to day, but invisible, merely presumed.

The bodies of those who commit suicide continue to fall periodically past the windows. The idea of joining this vertical ballet is no longer a last-ditch solution, but a scenario to consider here and now that imposes itself with more force than normal. We did what we could. We used all the ruses, all our talents. In vain. So, why not just let go?

Stop working. And fall.

No matter what happens now, the fall appears inevitable, no matter what turn things take.

For eight months, Solveig had not left her cubicle. Not even to help Théodore, whose blood had spilled onto the carpet, not even to attend the transformative surgery Clara had summoned the guild to, out of solidarity, and to make us understand that it was not one of her sadomasochistic experiments but, in fact, medical and biometric assistance.

Solveig, more than anyone else, had long been aware that the guild would sink into disorder, but the premonition was just a faint murmur to her, a possibility, a mere ornament in our tragedy. No matter what happens, her situation no longer allows for ambiguity: it already represents the worst possible catastrophe.

Solveig had studied pages of data on the global network and understood that her physical condition would gradually become untenable.

Confronted with her sudden and prolonged disappearance, we thought she was afraid of being held responsible for the death of the disembowelled young man.

On the space-time scale of the cafeteria, she was the first link in the chain reaction, and therefore what the responsibility algorithms called the 'primordial factor of the event.'

Before the video incriminating Clara appeared, the Copiers' investigation could have pointed the finger at any link in the chain, with a preference for the 'primordial factor' – that is, the triggering factor identified in the time and space of the tragedy.

We did not bother Solveig or try to give her advice. We imagined her concentrating on the data of the incident, running her machines to circumvent the obvious, using her free time to put together a desperate plan that would get her out of this tight spot.

But the truth was that Solveig couldn't care less about what happened in the cafeteria, the disembowelled young man, or the other members of the guild. Because, even cleared by an illusory counter-investigation, she knew she was doomed. Rather than studying the billions of pieces of legal information available on the global network, she was concentrating on an obscure subject that had few public traces on the networks. A subject we didn't know much about but that now affected her directly, and about which she needed to know each step, each physical and mental consequence, so as not to be surprised by one of the transformative phases she was going through. This mysterious, taboo subject was the reproduction of cats.

'Pregnant.' She whispered the word to Laszlo in front of the vending machine in the cafeteria. Even though she had heard it before and had a vague idea of its meaning, she quickly realized it would be difficult to define it or even imagine the condition it designated.

Because reproduction, in this world, has nothing to do with the reproduction of cats. It is, on the contrary, pure, which is to say handled entirely by machines. Agent Piotr, a few months earlier, had explained how humans liberated themselves from the reproduction of cats and put in place the institute system. Every twenty-eight days, agents voluntarily delivered to the reproduction airlock a viable ovum or a few millilitres of sperm. Agents who failed to provide the institute with the reproductive extract destined for the brewing of the genes of agent-kind received no censure or comment.

Next, in the inner workings of the machines, the genes were analyzed, blended, and purified, before being combined with eggs conceived in impenetrable labs. Reams of analysis on the global network explained how the genes were manipulated, but references to the reproduction of cats were fragmentary and evasive.

By inference, the agents knew approximately how a mammal went about obtaining an egg, but where that egg lived, how it grew without appropriate medical equipment, and, above all, what became of the male and female that produced it, no one knew; anyway, no one had to think about it.

Solveig had figured out that the egg didn't leave the female's body in the early days, as logic would suggest. On the contrary, she physically felt it gradually take hold inside her, felt her whole body change to accommodate it. Mentally, she became more aggressive, more aware of danger, bolting awake several times a night to find herself standing, in her hand the letter opener pointed in the direction of a sound that had disappeared.

Very quickly, her figure changed, and in just a few weeks, Solveig felt squeezed into her jumpsuit, so she was forced to take it off, remaining naked, alone in her cubicle, unable to go out and show herself in her condition to her colleagues. She who had always dedicated her life to purity of body and mind, considering her curves and hair as affronts to perfection, found herself deformed, her breasts enormous, blobs of fat lodged in places she didn't even know could contain them.

Then there was her stomach, which she had seen gently swell, little by little. First, she thought there was another fat deposit growing near her stomach. Without finding confirmation or repudiation on the global network, she had come to the oppressive conclusion that the egg would not come out, that it would grow there, in her distended abdomen, for how long she had no idea. This prospect had plunged her into a fathomless fright that fused the hideous image of a swollen body with the terror of not being able to survive this physical transformation.

And what is the point in surviving? Her body was no longer her body. It was a flaccid thing that sheathed and weighed on her. She constantly felt the revolting weight of her breasts on her ribs, a cat's teats on a cat's body, a bald cat, but a cat, not far from the human that no agent ever was. She forced herself to sleep, hoping that at least her mind would bring her back to a lost time when she was slim and light, but often her dreams wrapped her in an even more imposing envelope of skin and flesh, an unbounded mass that kept her from moving. Bloated, enormous, she was bumping into the partition walls of her cubicle, squeezed between the partitions as she had been in her jumpsuit, but unable to take them off, because these armoured walls were the last rampart that kept her from the eyes of the others, and those of the company, and as a result the street. Swelling and swelling some more, pushing against the partitions, her misshapen body was growing so fat that the cubicle exploded, and that was when she would wake up, sweating and in tears.

In other dreams, she saw herself as before, svelte, hovering above the ground like a little insect, but never free. Because the insect always circled around a monstrous creature, a mass of folds of yielding skin with no face, shuddering with turbulent waves accompanied by deep rumbles; the insect circled, unable to move away from the thing, inescapably attracted by her. A few moments after she woke up, Solveig noticed they weren't two distinct beings, just a single divided consciousness, condemned to heaviness and explosion, the person she used to be and the person she had become, with no possibility of choosing between the two.

But no matter what Solveig's dream was, what form it took, one thing remained unchanged: her personal tragedy had an additional character – a tiny speck of light that awaited in a corner of the dream space she visited – which she would have to deal with, which she felt obliged to protect and cherish, even though she knew it was responsible for her ordeal. It was this conviction that held her hand back when morning came, when the pain was too great, when the despair cut like a knife, and she would decide to eliminate what was growing inside her, the hidden source of her disfigurement and the humiliation that walked in step with her. Every time she tried, trembling as she cried, to expel this body inside her own body, she collapsed in helplessness, for reasons that no equation could show. With increasing rapidity, the end of the break would arrive without her having done anything. Forced to go back to work, she would let her powerlessness lose itself in the labyrinth of the data flows of this world.

After a few weeks, she wanted to get back in touch with Laszlo, on a closed network that was theirs alone. She told him what she was enduring day after day and asked him to provide food and comfort, which Laszlo agreed to, considering himself personally responsible for his colleague's condition.

For eight months, he helped her, out of solidarity, but also because the circumstances gave him a new idea he could use for his personal novel. Even if she had never caught him filming or recording their conversations, Solveig suspected that Laszlo's chivalry was not simply the result of his guilt or his friendship. It was curiosity. It's also what he called 'the ability of reality to make our lives less blind.' Because, more than any other experience ever had in this office, what was happening to Solveig was for Laszlo the ultimate outcome of his quest for truth and beauty. Without him having to leave the office, the reproduction of cats was available to him in detail, with a precision that the global network couldn't provide. Even if the outcome of this situation was lethal, for Solveig for sure, probably for him, his deviant mind told him that these long months learning what no one else had ever learned was worth their demise at their end.

Our guild had always sought, much more than power, the ultimate act of creation. We had directed the guild's strengths, justified its plotting, to transform the office into a place of beauty, despite the horrors and petty feelings that permeated it. And what Solveig and Laszlo were going to do, create a living being, without the help of the machines, appeared to be the outcome of this quest, like the most creative, the most desperate, and therefore the most beautiful act imaginable for an agent.

Because what could be more beautiful, for an agent, than to create another agent from scratch?

# 15.
# TOWER 35S, 122ND FLOOR,
# SECTOR Y1, CUBICLE 314

'It is 01:07 and the office is plunged in darkness. At this time of night, the carpet takes on a dark grey hue, as if colour were asleep as well, as if it were giving itself time to recover the strength required for its daytime radiance. The corridors are empty, but not everyone is sleeping, because these few hours dedicated to sleep are also dedicated to vigilance. It's the time when large-scale attacks are possible, the only moment when they can be launched outside the regulation fifteen minutes granted when the sun shines on this half of our planetary face.'

Laszlo whispers.

He holds his recorder in his hand, close to his mouth, and carefully places his bare feet on the floor of the empty office.

His senses are on alert, because, despite the care he is taking to make no noise, there is still the possibility that his presence will be remarked visually by an enemy system, like those presented by Douglas Beekle, the heat of his body, the weight of his bones, and the air he displaces becoming intimate traitors, stuck to him, exposing him as they define him.

So Laszlo avoids getting too close to the partitions and doors, and moves along a precise route, calculated by his personal machine, which reduces the likelihood of being detected in the corridors at night.

He walks another few metres in silence, and then stops in front of a cubicle.

'This is it. Where probability changes to certainty, and where truth crushes doubt. You who are listening to this message, this is the only thing you need to know about our world and those who populate it. I take a step toward the door of this unknown, and therefore enemy, cubicle, and no, you're not dreaming, no alarm is going off, no agent is growing agitated behind the armoured partition walls. I place my hand on the doorknob and there is no electric shock, no sound to suggest that my act of aggression has scared anyone. I turn the doorknob, which makes its small, characteristic sound, which all agents know to interpret as the signal of attack. You hear that? Nothing happens. And nothing happens when I push on the unlocked door, and I go in without encountering resistance. Nothing can happen because I have before my eyes truth and not doubt, doubt that grips an agent who thinks only of surviving. I am in cubicle 314, sector Y1, the 122nd floor, tower 35S, and you, who are listening to me, know that this is where the only thing that is important for an agent to know resides. Something there is no point in describing, as its mere evocation is not sufficient to attest to its existence. You too will have to see it to crush doubt with truth. This is why I am giving you the key to this discovery and the exact position of the chest it opens. I am in cubicle 314, sector Y1, the 122nd floor, tower 35S. Now I am leaving, hoping you will be the next to enter.'

Laszlo gently closes the door behind him and resumes his route through the silent corridors of the office, toward the west gallery, where the window turns red every night.

'It's not night, it's twilight. The twilight of our guild too weary to muster the strength to fight, because every one of its members is in danger.'

He arrives in front of Hick's cubicle and stays a good distance from the door, to avoid being spotted. His colleague is likely not sleeping, tortured by a tentacular algorithm the derivations of which lead to a more terrible fate each time.

'I am in front of Hick's cubicle,' Laszlo whispers, 'and for the first time since joining the office, Hick is truly afraid. And he is afraid because he is nice and efficient, and deduction has led him to infinite deadly ends. Hick understands that the trap we set for the smokers in the bathroom will hold off the Scarlet Brigade, but that there are other guilds, guilds that are investigating, guilds that are plotting, guilds that are drawing conclusions, guilds that are starting to wonder whether this great eccentric agent, dressed in an eye-catching tunic in purple velvet, is really what he claims to be. During these long months, reports circulated through the corridors of the office, rumour became probability, probability became a solid theory, even a certainty for some, now assured that the noisy replacement near the west window is absolutely not a Brigadier, but nothing at all, just the sad puppet of a minor guild who fooled the office for a bit of breathing room. Elsewhere, forces regrouped. The terms of the Solidarity Loan demanded it. The Veep Watchers conquered much of the northeast part of the floor – they believe this is the direction from which the Veeps arrive, in their flying vehicles, to honour us poor wretches with their presence. I am sure Solveig will soon receive a first courtesy visit. We don't know whether there are any Bookies left in the sectors that adjoin Hick's cubicle; their members have been methodically taken out by the Keepers guild. How long before the Keepers go after the Scarlet Brigade? Even more worrisome: the Kon-Trollers. Formerly one of the most powerful guilds in the office, it got into difficulty overnight. Its overwhelming superiority in number of cubicles was no longer of use to it. It had to attend to its borrowing potential by seizing adjacent cubicles, one after the other, during eight months of constant battle. Tonight, there is not one sector into which it has not stretched its formidable tentacles. When it thinks the time is right, at the signal of an invisible leader, at the twinkle of a dead star, at the order of a hypothetical calendar, it will swoop down on its adversaries. No one is safe. No one will be spared. So Hick is afraid. He is right to be afraid. He has become a seasoned agent in the past few months and knows that the attack is imminent, that no further shield of prestige will protect him, that he is vulnerable to the X number of guilds preparing to take his cubicle. The Scarlet Brigade, the Kon-Trollers, the Keepers, the Bookies, and so many others. Like all of us, Hick is alone tonight, and his fear is one of the glowing red colours that paint the portrait of our guild at twilight.'

Laszlo presses the pause button on his recorder and continues calmly on his way, leaving sector B and heading toward Clara's cubicle, where he stops. He releases the pause button and adds a string of sentences to the audio epitaph he is composing.

'The news that came down today leaves Clara no choice. If the defence for Agent Jubh has in its possession, as it claims, the video of the operation, tomorrow Clara will be found the sole agent responsible for the tragedy in the cafeteria. Her salvation will depend on the creation, during the night, of a case against members of her own guild. I am in front of Clara's cubicle. There is no sound coming from it, no sound of keys being hammered, no humming of a machine calculating. Clara is still, and she is waiting, but she undoubtedly isn't sleeping, taking advantage of her remaining hours to walk the carpet of the office. I want to push the door open and see for one last time the disfigured features of my long-time companion, with whom I used to be close enough to share her eccentricities. Tomorrow, her iconoclastic ideas of beauty and how to achieve it will be no more than data encrypted in the memory of those who knew her. Tomorrow, Clara will disappear, and with her an idea of an aesthetic that no agent will be able to develop anymore, because it is too personal and too incomprehensible. I'm going to press the pause button on my recorder, and I will spend the ground I cover during this time on hold thinking of Clara and what she brought us, often taking us in unimaginable directions, upending our bearings and making us, without us realizing it, superior beings who hover above the blind mass of agents, always further from the ugliness, archaism, and, basically, the condition of cats.'

Laszlo releases the pause button. He is now in front of Théodore's cubicle, but for a moment, his recorder captures only the silence of the office, because his thoughts are still with Clara.

Then his attention is turned toward his amputee colleague, and Laszlo searches for the words to describe him without his amused disdain for him coming through on the recording.

'I am in front of Théodore's cubicle,' he says.

But a deep silence follows, which he decides to maintain, as a touch of irony that will shed light on the words that will follow.

'If the guild disappears tomorrow and he alone survives the looming carnage, saved by Clara's providential operation, he will continue to spin like a moon on its axis before being struck down by his own eccentricity. His greatest feat will have been managing to convince those who were watching him that someone as unlikely as him was a member of a guild as powerful as the Brigadiers. It is at the same time his victory, his trophy, and his death sentence.'

Laszlo frowns in consternation as he presses pause, disappointed not to have been able to lie better, but at the same time relieved to have managed to say anything at all.

His last step is Solveig's cubicle; he knows she won't be sleeping either, fearing confronting the repulsive image of herself transformed into a pile of fatty, oozing flesh.

'Behind this door lives the most horrible and the most sublime thing an agent can create. I am in front of Solveig's cubicle, the sun will rise soon, and this is the moment I have chosen to bring our fates to a conclusion that could not be anticipated, even by machines. We who have lived in dignity, we will disappear the same way, if all goes well, at the end of a day that will seal the great task we have taken on.'

Laszlo taps on the door of Solveig's cubicle, using a previously agreed-upon rhythm. He hears the weak squeak of the distressed wheels of the approaching chair, then a tapped rhythm answers him. He enters the cubicle.

'What are you doing here at this time of night?' Solveig asks, her eyes red with tears.

'It's not night,' Laszlo answers. 'It's twilight. And tomorrow the sun of a new day will rise on our lives.'

Solveig, her hands on her swollen belly, doesn't seem to be listening to him. Her furtive gesture, between two stifled sobs, is ambiguous. Laszlo can't tell whether it's despair, disgust, or joy.

'You want to touch it?' she asks. 'One last time?'

Laszlo smiles, and the horrible assumption Solveig has just expressed doesn't seem to affect him. He reaches toward Solveig's stomach and places his hand on it gently without taking his eyes off his colleague.

'Do you remember a conversation we had a long time ago?' he asks, still smiling. 'A conversation about the Veeps?'

'No,' Solveig answers, absent. 'Do you feel it moving? Do you feel this thing moving inside me? It's alive, Laszlo. How does it manage to live in there?'

'It was a forgettable conversation,' Laszlo goes on. 'You told me you didn't believe Cily Vinière existed. Do you remember what I said that day?'

'Yes,' Solveig says, not understanding how Laszlo can talk about general news given the situation.

'We never talked about it again, but what I told you that day was true. I met Cily Vinière, for real, and she knows me. Maybe you're not reading the general news feed anymore, but she will be here tomorrow. Cily Vinière-Banks. She will land on the roof of our tower to meet an employee representative.'

'What difference does that make, Laszlo?' Solveig asks, crying. 'What will it change, this woman landing I don't know how many floors above our heads? We broke the law. We're criminals. You want us to go on the global network with a grievance that tells our story? It's over, Laszlo. There is only one solution left. I can feel it. This thing is going to come out of my body soon. I don't know how, but it will do it and probably kill me in the process. We can't go back. We have seen too much. We have learned too much. Now we have to decide. Either I die so this thing takes my place, I don't know how, and you let it grow up here, in this cubicle, even though it seems impossible. Or we take immediate measures so that another crime hides the first.'

Laszlo is still smiling, his hand resting on Solveig's stomach, feeling the sudden movements of the thing she is carrying, the genetic product of the two of them, without the intervention of the machines, a pure creation of two agents becoming a third.

'There is another solution,' he says. 'Because I know of a passage. In sector Z.'

'Sector Z is deserted,' Solveig says. 'There is nothing there, just giant plants and insects as big as your fist.'

'No, Solveig. Just because everyone thinks there's nothing there, and just because they tell us there's nothing there, doesn't mean it's true. It's just a probability, and any probability can be disproven through experience. We know that better than anyone.'

Solveig sniffs, runs her hand over her smooth head, and starts to take an interest in what Laszlo is saying.

'There's a door in sector Z,' he continues. 'It's an old door, which agents must have used in the past, but the purpose of which has been forgotten, along with its existence. It is hidden behind wild vegetation that grows there and that has covered it up right down to the memory of it. But I found it. I got through the vegetation, and I placed my hands on the metal it's made of. It's shiny metal, where you can see your image reflected, nothing like the dull metal our cubicles are made with, which absorbs all the light to hide its strength. The door must have been put there at the same time as this tower and the 8-Char Door. Our ancestors installed it, and like everything our ancestors installed, they used it for something.'

'For what?' asks Solveig, who, in her distress, has decided to believe this unbelievable tale.

'I don't know what the agents called the door back then,' Laszlo says, 'so I named it. I call it the Up and Down Door. Because, yes, Solveig, it's a door that can take you from floor to floor in the tower, to every floor, and even to the roof. That's why all is not lost. Because tomorrow, when Cily Vinière's aircraft touches down on our tower, we won't be prisoners here awaiting our death. We will be on the roof, and we will welcome her, and she will listen to us. I know she will listen to us, because like I told you months ago, and like I just told you now, even if you didn't believe me, not then and not tonight, I'll say it again: I know Cily Vinière really well.'

# III.
# GRAVITY

The tea has been drunk, the hot plates put away, and the screens glow this morning, just like they glowed yesterday and will glow tomorrow.

It is five o'clock, and the agents get down to work.

The generator in the basement sends thousands of kilowatts through the tower's electrical column, which, equitably, is dispersed into personal and collective devices, lighting, screens, computers, air-flow switching modules, nanomachines.

The outdoor sensors feed the algorithms that generate local news according to the location of the cubicles, the level of sunlight on the floor, the latitude of the towers, each agent being pleased to read this morning, like all other mornings, news prepared just for them to which they alone have access.

Each agent is unique.

They execute a specific task. They have access to data feeds they alone are responsible for. It's their pride, their dignity, and their responsibility, which only an unwavering ethic and dedication enable them to bear for the time between the 8-Char Door and the bacteriological tomb.

We are unique. Every one of us.

This is why the company respects us, and by showing ourselves to be worthy of this respect, we can congratulate ourselves on this uniqueness.

The system is designed this way, a shiny link in the history of human worlds, an infinite loop fuelled endlessly by mutual respect.

We respect the company because the company respects us.

And the company respects us because we respect it.

It's the vital chain of modern reality, perfect, irrefutable, the precious movement that lifts us above the condition of cats, just like our ancestors lifted us above the sterile ground.

When we joined the office, we agreed not to break the chain, to protect it, to worship work as it deserves, so that our work can bring us the dignity we will have thereby earned.

Not following the rules of the office, breaking its laws, means exposing ourselves to the fall and to dishonour. Sometimes we let ourselves deviate slightly from the straight and narrow of purity, but we do it with full knowledge, with a gaping wound of painful shame in the pit of our stomach, threatening to spread its gangrene and to turn us into moving waste, good only for the street, too rotten for one of the particles that make us up to even be recycled in any way.

There has never been an agent, in the history of the modern world, who argued in their defence that they were unaware of the company laws or the sentences handed down for violating them.

We live for these laws. And if we break them, it's not to question them, but out of self-loathing for we who are unable to espouse their perfection.

We struggle against the weight that bends and breaks us, plasters us to the carpet where we are trampled by those who are more worthy. We fight to be tall. We fight to stand straight. But the temptation, in every moment of every battle, to give up and let ourselves fall, is always with us and haunts us, a dark companion cloaked in shadow, who walks in our footsteps, slips into the memory of our gestures, and sometimes offers to guide them, a despairing soldier on the lower road, and in the gleam of eyes in which we can make out our silhouettes, our own silhouettes, we who are without hope or power, dust thrown into the force of headwinds, with no limb, organ, or will able to resist the natural power that is crushing us.

At the extreme of this abandonment of self, there is the street, and dismissal, the logical rather than brutal end that makes official and public an already personal and private shame.

We strike our keyboards. Slowly, then faster and faster, as the hour advances and our minds wake up. In the office, the sound of keys being pressed sounds at first like raindrops drumming on the windows of the tower as a shower passes, then becomes a continuous patter that is our companion for the day, a coat of sound cloaking the office, clusters of rhythmic data we sometimes get lost in the depths of as we try to understand its elusive logic, accelerations moving from one sector to another as if an algorithm governs their movement – which is probably the case – merging waves of tapping, born without logic and dying the same way, disappearing in one place to reappear a few cubicles down, echoes of tones that answer without listening to each other, musical symptoms of the state of the office, often much more insightful than the horoscopes that display on our screens.

Beginning at 05:02, on the global network, in the midst of the quantity of information that designs the world, a lone object is moving. A simple polygon, a discrete piece of data, that slowly moves before our eyes without attracting attention.

The minutes go by, and as we toil the first three hours of our day, the shape evolves, it swells, gorges itself, feeds on its own discreteness and our disappointed expectations, and by about 06:30, it has become a swollen, purulent, informational object, even more worrisome because it doesn't exist and no one sees it.

Our guild in particular becomes absorbed in contemplating this absence, both fascinated and fearful, incredulous about this twist of fate that upends our predictions and triggers new worried, silent questioning.

This invisible object – we are unable to decide whether its existence or non-existence would be more terrible to take – is the announcement of Clara's dismissal, which everyone expects, but which still has not been disseminated by one of these official memos that we are required to read, because we don't know whether it concerns us or not.

The evidence is in. Clara must fall.

But she doesn't fall.

She is in her cubicle. She is working.

Her asymmetrical face is an ocean tossed by massive waves. Those who know her know that the muscular vibrations that distort her features are not just spasms but often emotions being rendered in a facial language we don't understand. For any other agent, however, Clara's face remains a riddle you quickly look away from, convinced of its absurdity; looking at the video captures that show us oceans, we do not waste time searching for the feeling symbolized by a small ripple nor the emotion that generates a crest of foam. It's an ocean, a ripple, or foam. That's all. The oceans and Clara's face mean nothing. They are just there, mysterious productions of a nature that is just as mysterious.

It is 06:47, and the discrete polygon in orbit around verified information is so imposing that it starts to attract other hazy elements. It radiates and forms a pointillist cloud around it. Sometimes, one of the particles escapes and joins another screen, on another workstation. The parts thus created divide in turn to form a thick cloud of volatile rumour, running through the networks, multiplied and melted into the particular interpretations of the info-system in which it is evolving.

We like stories.

And rumours are the most joyful of stories, because, unlike verified information, they take the form we want, malleable and docile – at times to respond to our unmet expectations, at others to change into an immaterial guide that takes us by the hand and leads us toward lands of hope, where we forget that we are the ones who created this reassuring construction, to no longer be surrounded by the devastating rigour of certain, exact information.

Clara waits.

She is absorbed by her task and tries to close, unread, the messages on the general channel that are displayed and that discuss theories that could explain why the company has not yet initiated its dismissal procedure.

Laszlo is delighted. With the announcement not coming, he has gained time and freedom to act. At 07:06, he opens a private channel with Hick.

[chan#W889] LASZLO: Time is running out.

[chan#W889] HICK: That depends on for whom.

[chan#W889] LASZLO: For all of us. For Clara.

[chan#W889] HICK: Clara would like time to stop, I think. Not have it run out.

[chan#W889] LASZLO: It concerns her too. I have a plan.

The cursor blinks. No words appear. Hick waits.

[chan#W889] LASZLO: Today is the day everything has to be resolved, as you know.

[chan#W889] LASZLO: You're in danger too.

[chan#W889] HICK: I know.

[chan#W889] LASZLO: I explained to Solveig how it will work. You have to meet up with her when I give you the word, and you will leave.

[chan#W889] HICK: What are you talking about?

[chan#W889] HICK: Where are we going?

[chan#W889] LASZLO: She'll explain once you're with her.

[chan#W889] LASZLO: Once you're with her, you'll understand how urgent it is.

[chan#W889] HICK: If I'm going to agree to follow her, I have to know more.

[chan#W889] LASZLO: You will die if you stay here waiting.

[chan#W889] LASZLO: What more do you need to know?

Again, no activity.

Hick thinks.

He is aware of the rumours too. Particularly the ones about him that claim he is no more a Brigadier than Josh McGuilick. Even that he is nothing. A mere scarecrow brandished by a crafty but weakly guild. An easy target, vulnerable. A replacement like any other who deserves the same fate as any other when the end of the month comes.

The announcement of Clara's dismissal, in a few seconds or a few hours, will be the signal that the hunt is on. The Copiers' report will reveal the ties between the members of our guild and, our anonymity shattered, will make us potential prey for the other groups in the office.

[chan#W889] HICK: When will it go down?

[chan#W889] LASZLO: Soon. Wait for my signal.

[chan#W889] LASZLO: And be ready.

[chan#W889] LASZLO: We will all be in danger, so everyone has to ensure their own protection.

[chan#W889] LASZLO: You have to be able to hold your own for a few minutes.

[chan#W889] HICK: Without a weapon?

[chan#W889] LASZLO: Without a weapon.


Laszlo closes the channel, hoping Hick won't change his mind.

Sometimes, some agents, particularly the younger ones, refuse to fight and let themselves be defeated. Not necessarily because they are weak and think they have no chance, but because, during their first skirmish, they imagine what their existence here will be until the end: a long series of battles for survival. This dark outlook overwhelms them and makes them give up, horrified at the idea of never knowing anything other than fear.

But Hick isn't young. If he didn't give up when faced with the instructor, maybe he won't give up faced with flesh-and-blood people like him. No smarter or stronger than him. Hick is stubborn and impertinent. These two faults could be assets for our guild today.

At 07:53, the soothing clatter of keyboards stops. The office lights go out, even though the light of the invisible sun continues to shine.

A special message appears on our screens, making Clara's shame official and public.

SPECIAL MESSAGE – DISMISSAL
In light of evidence provided by the Copiers guild as part of investigation MD66373, the company is prepared to render its decision regarding the events that occurred eight months ago in the cafeteria on the 122nd floor.

As required by our Code of Criminal Procedure, the evidence offered by the defence will be available for consultation on the global network as of the next break, at 08:00.

This evidence formally accuses an agent on this floor, and the company will now execute the punishment set out in our Labour Code.

#

EMPLOYEE DISMISSED:
Name: Clara
Location: sector A2\cubicle 17
Reason(s): manslaughter (art. 8), illegal practice of surgery endangering her own and another's life (art. 472), damage to company property (art. 16), leaving the scene of an accident (art. 39).

#

The above-mentioned employee no longer works for the company or for any other company, as of the receipt of this message. She is therefore asked to vacate her cubicle and report immediately to the 8-Char Door.
END OF MESSAGE

The office rejoices and trembles.

We just tremble; while we have felt it in the past, this time we cannot share in the feeling sweeping over agents on the floor.

It's the same thing every time an employee is dismissed. A sense of honour and pride. The immense satisfaction of not being that employee and having been more valiant so we can keep our jobs longer than them. Because we feel more valuable as more agents are dismissed.

It's the horrible arithmetic of the office, which prevents us from feeling pity and requires us to delight in the misfortune of others.

It is our only landmark in this world in motion where honour and pride hide and are out of reach. If no one were ever punished for their offences, how would we know that we are rewarded for our victories? Our permanent victory is the fact of being there. And not on the street.

We don't panic but understand that now, at 07:56, the day has just begun – the final day of our guild.

No one says anything on our private network. No funerary column draws a line through our screens, no message for Clara, who we know is no longer looking at the data that describes a world she has just been excluded from.

There are four minutes left before the break, and Laszlo hopes he will be able to intercept his colleague in time, hold her in his arms before she reaches the 8-Char Door and disappears through it, hopes as well that she won't decide to move her sentence forward and will wait until eight o'clock to leave her cubicle.

But Clara's disfigured face is already advancing along the office's grey carpet.

She is there and not there, with the dual status that only a dismissed agent acquires, for the few minutes' walk that separates her from the 8-Char Door.

When an agent is dismissed, they stand and walk straight to meet their end, a ghost like those who stream past the windows, in freefall and serene in the midst of the shards of glass.

No armed force comes to get you out of your cubicle. No company representative comes to tell you personally that you have been dismissed. When you are dismissed, you take responsibility in the same way you took it in the months and years spent working, so that a greater dishonour is not added to the already insurmountable one that is being endured.

Clara stands up straight and advances, watched by dozens of cameras that conduct surveillance on agents and that broadcast live on the global network the cathartic images of her final walk.

It is 07:59 when she reaches sector A1 and stops in front of the 8-Char Door, the expulsion indicator light blinking like the shiny reflection of a sword ready to come down on her neck. She turns back and takes a last look at the straight aisles of the office, the worn carpet, the armoured cubicles, and the tubular alignment of the fluorescent lights now turned off that were her sky for all these years.

At the same moment, Laszlo has his hand on the doorknob of his cubicle, muscles tensed, eye glued to the clock on his screen counting down the final seconds before the break. If he were not obsessed by the series of movements that would pitch him outside at exactly eight o'clock to rush toward the 8-Char Door, he would regret not having warned Clara earlier, not having kept her abreast of the plan that would save them all today. But that scene is playing out in another possible universe, where Clara is sitting on her chair when the announcement of her dismissal appears and her bizarre features form what we know to be a smile. It is in another reality that she was warned by Laszlo that she no longer needs to walk toward the street, where there is a different end to her life, which has already been wiped from the company's synthetic memories. It is also in another space-time that Laszlo does not need to rush into the corridors of the office when his clock finally says 08:00.

The sounds of footsteps, the rustle of clothing, doors slammed ahead and behind, revealing new activity. In the four corners of the floor, agents start to attack, simultaneously, as if it were the obvious thing to do. Wars are declared. It's time for all hell to break loose.

The final battle we feared and anticipated starts with a huge explosion in sector K that reverberates throughout the office. The attack begins. Grenades start flying, gunfire rings out.

Laszlo heads down the central aisle, ignoring the plumes of smoke rising from the ends of the corridors that he passes as fast as he can. Cubicles open, spitting out furious agents or deadly projectiles that fall thick and fast around him. He swings his arms in wide arcs as he runs and thinks at times that he is touching the anonymous bodies of colleagues throwing themselves on him. The bodies fall, and he steps over them. The partition walls sway; he avoids them. Nothing can divert his frantic race toward Clara, whom he has lost from sight now that he isn't in front of his screen. Yet there she is, at the end of the aisle, behind the smoke and the rage. Cries rise up from sector K – Théodore's sector – and from sector M2 – where the bathrooms are – and yet more from the west side of the office, where there have been no attacks for years.

But today is a special day, the day of the big battle, and the power alliances formed by the end of this day will shape the office in a new thermodynamic equilibrium. Before the equilibrium, there must be chaos and the crushing of some forces by others with more power or luck. Agents can take part in the unrest or are condemned to be pulverized if they stay on the sidelines.

Laszlo passes by sectors E1 and F1. Some fifty metres away, he has spotted Clara, facing the 8-Char Door, getting ready to be swallowed up by it. He keeps running but sees no point in shouting because the commotion around him is deafening and wipes out words and thoughts. To the west, the chants of the Scarlet Brigade rise up and add to the mayhem.

Laszlo is no longer thinking; he is running. Straight toward the door that has revealed a metal alcove, human-sized, first and last vehicle for any agent who doesn't want to die on the job, source of life and hope for those who emerge from it and of shame for those who enter.

Clara is in the alcove, a dull, dark coffin in the depths of which she already seems dead. She pivots and faces the office, the main aisle, and Laszlo, who continues to run and screams:

'Don't go! Don't go!'

An even more powerful explosion than the previous ones shakes the floor. The blast spreads through the air conditioning ducts, blows through the partition walls, hurls atom against atom, flattening to the ground anything that is not solidly attached.

Laszlo's feet lift off from the carpet, his legs slice the air as if he were still running. Carried on the blast of the explosion, he feels himself accelerate and then crash to the ground. He rolls on the carpet and thinks of his camera, tucked in his jacket pocket. Did it withstand the shock?

He is lying on his stomach. His hands frantically pat his jacket looking for his camera, which they find and train on the 8-Char Door, and on Clara.

Laszlo shouts again, 'Don't go!' while pressing the record button and checking the viewfinder to see whether it is in focus.

The image is blurry. It takes a few tenths of a second for the camera's automatic focus to correct it. Clara appears, dazzling in the middle of a sky of digital specks moving from dark grey to black. She doesn't look at Laszlo. She looks at the lens, and her inhuman face contorts to form what we know is a smile.

'Don't go!'

He is just five metres from his colleague, a dark silhouette fading into the shadowy corner, but Laszlo is screaming at his camera's miniature screen.

Clara does not relax her singular smile. She takes out an object from her pocket, while around her the smoke and noise just keep intensifying.

She keeps staring at the lens and plants a scalpel in her carotid artery, which she severs with the same gesture. With all the time she has spent studying human anatomy and practising surgery, how could she possibly miss the artery?

Laszlo starts to regret that Clara is not as stupid as Théodore, so she could botch it, as he did, and survive at least a few minutes more. He tries to get up while his right hand holds the camera so that Clara remains in the frame.

In thirty frames a second, it records her movement as follows: pulling the scalpel from her throat, blood gushing from the wound and splashing the door jamb of the alcove to the rhythm of her heartbeat. It also records the perfect trajectory in the arc of a circle of the instrument that, from the other side of the neck, pierces the skin and the twin artery.

Clara is still smiling as her legs give out from under her, and she hits the partition wall, losing more blood than anyone can sustain. She is still smiling when the sliding 8-Char Door closes on her doomed image.

It is 08:05, and until 08:06 Laszlo no longer hears the fury being unleashed around him, the cubicles exploding, the fanatical chants, the agents screaming, mown down.

Something round rolls along the carpet and comes to a stop in front of him.

He snatches it and throws it down the side corridor.

A grenade.

It explodes in the middle of sector A5, setting off a deep rumble followed by horrified cries.

Laszlo gets up and turns off the camera.

Smoke has filled almost the entire sector. Time to go. Here he is an easy target. Hundreds of computers spent months analyzing and calculating acceptable attacks, useful actions, necessary manoeuvres, but this no longer has any importance. Nothing more counts today, no more alliances or strategies, protections or agreements. In this sort of chaos, the rule seems obvious: agents who don't know how to survive will perish.

Laszlo puts his camera away and rushes toward sector K.

The office is unrecognizable.

The open doors of cubicles slow his progress, while thick, suffocating smoke spreads from the fires.

Some cubicles are on fire, and the synthetic carpet is slowly burning near the scorched bodies of agents that the acid gasses have not yet disintegrated.

Laszlo runs as fast as he can, jumps over the dead and the wounded who are groaning, picks up whatever he can, weapons, projectiles, which he drops a few metres further on, once their ammunition has been spent in the direction of the furtive shadows threatening to mow him down.

He rounds the corner of sector K and the bathrooms, and arrives, at 08:08, near Théodore's cubicle.

The corridor seems calm, but Laszlo spots a section of wire mesh above the north partition wall of his colleague's cubicle. It's a roof, the sort of protection deployed to shield him from the grenades.

Laszlo concludes from it that Théodore got scared when he heard the explosion at eight o'clock, or else he has really been attacked, and maybe that attack is ongoing.

He searches the adjacent cubicles and, indeed, a miniature roaming camera is installed above the bathroom door across from Théodore's cubicle. Luckily, Laszlo has arrived between two waves. The assailants must be rearming or devising a tactic to capture the coveted cubicle. He has to act now, before the next assault.

'Théodore! It's Laszlo! Open the door!'

Around the deserted bathroom and cafeteria, everything is calm, and Laszlo's voice resonates. Unless his eardrums were perforated by the blast of a grenade that exploded too close to him, Théodore must have heard it.

Regardless, it's a risk to be taken, because the statistics, while roughly calculated by a mere human, are favourable. They won't be in a minute.

Laszlo leaps into the corridor, followed by the eye of the miniature camera. He throws himself against the locked door of Théodore's cubicle and dislocates his right shoulder.

'Jesus, Théodore! Open the door! It's Laszlo!'

The miniature camera freezes, the bathroom door opens a crack, and a dark shape appears in the doorway.

The sound of the electronic bolt can be heard. Laszlo pushes the door before Théodore opens it, and he dives inside the cubicle, dodging the bullets from the gun across the way.

Laszlo hears them ricochet off the reinforced titanium of the now-closed door.

'I'm so sorry, Laszlo,' Théodore says. 'But I thought it was a trap. You know, they have things like that now. Devices that imitate voices.'

'So why did you let me in, you idiot?' Laszlo says, putting his shoulder back in place.

'Well, I don't know. They don't imitate them all that well…I think.'

Laszlo doesn't even listen to his colleague's reasoning and heads directly toward his computer to check the time – 08:10 – and open a private channel with Solveig.

[chan#X33374] THÉODORE: It's Laszlo.

[chan#X33374] THÉODORE: I'm at Théodore's workstation.

[chan#X33374] THÉODORE: Are you okay?

Nothing.

Théodore approaches and reads over Laszlo's shoulder.

'What's going on, Laszlo?' he asks. 'Why is everyone killing each other?'

'I had forgotten how ugly you are since the operation,' Laszlo answers calmly.

[chan#X33374] SOLVEIG: I'm okay.

[chan#X33374] SOLVEIG: I put up the wire mesh,

[chan#X33374] SOLVEIG: but it's as if no one is interested in my cubicle.

Laszlo frowns and pauses to calculate the likelihood that this is true.

Today, everyone is interested in every cubicle. The fact that Solveig's hasn't been attacked is a statistical anomaly:

95 per cent: Solveig's cubicle has been captured and another agent answered.

4 per cent: Through some miracle, Solveig's cubicle hasn't been attacked.

1 per cent: Some other highly improbable solution.

'Théodore,' he says. 'Can you step back? I want to ask Solveig a personal question.'

Théodore opens wide his haggard eyes, makes a resentful face, but backs up to check that the wire mesh is solidly attached to the partition walls. Given his grave face, Laszlo realizes he has offended him, but he doesn't care, and types on the keyboard.

[chan#X33374] THÉODORE: I need to know that it's really you.

[chan#X33374] THÉODORE: So, just answer one question:

[chan#X33374] THÉODORE: What's in your stomach?

Théodore whistles, his hands clasped behind his back, to signify his irritation. He is leaning against a partition wall and doesn't take his eyes off Laszlo. He waits for his colleague to notice his disapproval.

Without losing his cool, Laszlo hops on the desk and swats at the wire mesh that covers the cubicle. Théodore starts, almost falls, but has time to see that Laszlo has dislodged a grenade with its pin out that was just thrown at them.

'Christ, watch out, Théodore,' Laszlo screams. 'Quit daydreaming and keep an eye on the cubicle!'

Théodore stands up straight, trying to remain dignified, but doesn't know what to say and, contrite, stares at the wire mesh while Laszlo sits back down in front of the screen. Solveig's answer has appeared.

It's 08:12.

[chan#X33374] SOLVEIG: An agent.

[chan#X33374] THÉODORE: Okay.

[chan#X33374] THÉODORE: I have just enough time to go back to my cubicle.

[chan#X33374] THÉODORE: Stay online.

[chan#X33374] THÉODORE: We're going to go over the final details,

[chan#X33374] THÉODORE: and we leave at 09:00.

[chan#X33374] SOLVEIG: During work hours...

[chan#X33374] THÉODORE: Yes.

[chan#X33374] SOLVEIG: Anyway...

[chan#X33374] SOLVEIG: Okay.

Laszlo waits a few seconds in front of the screen, to ensure that the lines of this guilty discussion have disappeared.

Then he heads toward the door.

'They won't attack now,' he says to Théodore. 'They can't stay in the bathroom after the break. But the attack isn't over. I'll come back at 11:15, and we'll ride it out. If we survive today, everything will change. We have to hold our own, Théodore. Do you understand?'

Théodore looks serious, and suddenly he appears much less ridiculous than normal. Laszlo attributes this impression to the fact that he is leaning against a partition wall, so his unbalanced body doesn't need to be in rotation to stay upright. Standing straight, a sombre expression on his face, Théodore almost looks like a normal agent.

'Laszlo,' Théodore says. 'What exactly is going on? It's not just us. The whole office is trying to kill each other. Why?'

'I don't know,' Laszlo says. 'See you in a bit.'

It's 08:13 when Laszlo throws opens the cubicle door and rushes into the corridor. There are sprays of gunfire, but, surprised by

Laszlo's speed, the assailants have not had time to take aim, and only the armoured door of Théodore's cubicle sustains new damage.

The office is even more of a disaster.

The smoke is dissipating in several sectors.

Laszlo doesn't dare imagine the chaos that must have reigned in this part of the office, where visibility of just a few centimetres must have favoured instinct over strategy, spontaneous violence over premeditated acts.

In the partially burnt-out corridors, the cleaning clouds disintegrate the sprawled bodies, and pools of blood run under closed doors.

It's the great purge, Laszlo thinks, without slowing his pace, the day of an end and a beginning, one that will ultimately decide who has been lucky and powerful enough to control this place for years to come. It's judgment day, when all agents – no exceptions – must respond with skill and courage.

But when he finally reaches the corridor of sector U1, the location of his armoured cubicle, which is visibly intact despite the battle that was waged here too, he thinks that this day, basically, is not so different from any other. A simple change in the time scale. A concentration of events – forces that crush others, energies that shift – that would have taken place no matter what, in a different way, diluted in the dreary frieze of days, but the outcome of which would have led to the same new thermodynamic balance, stable enough to provide the office with fleeting tranquility, until the next upset.

He enters his cubicle at 08:14, locks the door behind him, and immediately sits down at his workstation like other agents in the office must be doing, victimizers and victims, members of guilds or Underlins. In a few seconds, the break will be over, and they have to get back to work.

Laszlo's machine hums and displays three-dimensional rows of alphanumeric data.

Market values are stable. The economy is booming. Growth is exponential.

Companies post their results. Astronomical profits are immediately and automatically injected into businesses in bankruptcy.

Economic structures expand, others waver and collapse.

The modern world is working.

To perfection.

And we are its witnesses.


[chan#W889] LASZLO: We need to talk.

[chan#W889] HICK: Jesus, what's going on?

[chan#W889] HICK: I've been trying to reach everyone the entire break.

[chan#W889] HICK: No one answered.

[chan#W889] HICK: Where are the others?

[chan#W889] LASZLO: Clara is gone.

[chan#W889] LASZLO: The others are okay.

[chan#W889] LASZLO: I think.

[chan#W889] LASZLO: And you?

[chan#W889] HICK: It was insane!

[chan#W889] HICK: I don't know how many of them were out there.

[chan#W889] HICK: I think I killed at least three.

[chan#W889] HICK: They all came at me at once.

[chan#W889] LASZLO: Everyone came at everyone.

[chan#W889] LASZLO: It's not just you.

[chan#W889] HICK: I don't give a shit.

[chan#W889] HICK: You have to help me during the next break.

[chan#W889] HICK: I got lucky this time, but they look like they mean it.

[chan#W889] HICK: They were singing like lunatics.

[chan#W889] HICK: They were throwing themselves against the door with everything they had.

[chan#W889] HICK: I won't hold out another fifteen minutes.

[chan#W889] LASZLO: You won't have to.

[chan#W889] HICK: What do you mean?

[chan#W889] LASZLO: We're leaving.

[chan#W889] LASZLO: I know a way to the roof.

[chan#W889] LASZLO: In forty-five minutes, we'll head there and meet up with Cily Vinière.

[chan#W889] HICK: You're out of your mind!

[chan#W889] LASZLO: We don't have a choice.

[chan#W889] LASZLO: Either we leave or we'll be killed here.

[chan#W889] HICK: This is bullshit.

[chan#W889] HICK: I won't leave my cubicle during working hours.

[chan#W889] HICK: It's out of the question.

[chan#W889] HICK: I don't want to end up like Clara.

[chan#W889] LASZLO: Jesus, Hick! How do you want to end up?

[chan#W889] LASZLO: Torn to shreds by a grenade?

[chan#W889] LASZLO: They won't stop until they seize your cubicle, do you get it?

[chan#W889] LASZLO: It's over!

[chan#W889] LASZLO: If we stay here, we're dead!

[chan#W889] HICK: If we leave our station, we're dead.

[chan#W889] LASZLO: Maybe not!

[chan#W889] LASZLO: Look at the odds!

[chan#W889] LASZLO: We have a chance on the roof.

[chan#W889] LASZLO: It's slim, but we have a chance.

[chan#W889] LASZLO: Here we have none.

Laszlo is exasperated but manages to control himself. Hick is stubborn, he knows, but all is not yet lost.

And yet, seconds pass with no answer.

It's 08:18, and time is running out.

While waiting for Hick to decide, Laszlo pictures the possibility of his refusal and runs his personal statistical tool. Not his machine, but his brain, because this type of calculation has to remain secret, and no device on the global network can have access to it.

For a moment, it crosses his mind that the system may also have access to agents' brains and monitor their thoughts, reams of data that display on the screens that other agents monitor. Maybe even on our own screens, everyone monitoring everyone without realizing it, roaming a global network that is nothing more than the sum of our thoughts, translated and interconnected.

After all, why not? Our minds are so rudimentary compared with the technologies that the modern world has developed. Why would it be hard for machines to observe and understand it? They say our brainwaves travel through our skull and radiate a few centimetres around our heads. And what if, aside from the cameras observing us, other sensors were built into our cubicles to listen to our thoughts, analyze them, and disseminate them?

Laszlo launches another statistical calculation in his head.

If the machines know his plan, why is he still here, trying to execute it? Why has no dismissal notice appeared on the screens to throw him out of the office?

At 99.99 per cent, the odds are clear: providing the evidence that Laszlo is up to no good would force the machines to reveal that they are monitoring our minds. But if this is the case, and it has not been made public so far, there is no reason it would be now.

If they are watching us, the machines will deal with the deserters once they are on the roof. They will catch them red-handed. Not before.

[chan#W889] HICK: And the others?
[chan#W889] HICK: Are they on board?
[chan#W889] LASZLO: All of them.

Hick is caving. Laszlo is sure of it.

He hasn't been out of the institute for long. For him, statistical laws are still the only laws to be trusted. The instinct for survival has not yet consumed him. Faint probabilities that materialize against all expectations have not yet shaken his faith in numbers. If he respects logic, he will accept.

[chan#W889] HICK: Not me.

[chan#W889] HICK: Do what you want, but I'm going to work until
11:15.

[chan#W889] HICK: If you're still here then, I'll follow you.

[chan#W889] LASZLO: Okay.

[chan#W889] LASZLO: I'll be back in touch.


Laszlo is disappointed. This is a sharp new reminder that nothing
is a given and that faint probabilities can materialize against all expectations. Statistics never offer complete certainty, and the rates always
hover around the theoretical threshold of 99.99 per cent, but there
is still the possibility that nothing will go as anticipated. And today,
that faint probability seems to be repeating itself too often.

But Laszlo doesn't consider changing his plan and refuses even
to imagine Théodore replacing Hick on the team that will go up to
the roof. You can play with statistics, but trusting Théodore is no
longer playing: it's suicide. Despite the desire for death that fills
him, his pride won't allow him to owe that death to the idiocy of
his twirling colleague. He opens a private channel with Solveig.

[chan#SQ8837] LASZLO: Change of plans. We leave at 11:15.

[chan#SQ8837] SOLVEIG: Ah.

[chan#SQ8837] LASZLO: Hick refuses to leave during work hours.

[chan#SQ8837] SOLVEIG: I understand.

[chan#SQ8837] LASZLO: Be ready at 11:18.

[chan#SQ8837] LASZLO: It'll take him a few minutes to get to you.

[chan#SQ8837] SOLVEIG: Laszlo?

[chan#SQ8837] LASZLO: Yes?

[chan#SQ8837] SOLVEIG: And Théodore?

[chan#SQ8837] SOLVEIG: You didn't mention Théodore.

[chan#SQ8837] LASZLO: I'll take care of Théodore.

[chan#SQ8837] LASZLO: You just wait for Hick.

[chan#SQ8837] SOLVEIG: Give him the map of sector Z.

[chan#SQ8837] LASZLO: Run and don't look back.

[chan#SQ8837] SOLVEIG: Right.

The clocks on the screens read 08:27.

The office's usual calm has been restored, but as is often the case, the calm is a cover for violence, that momentary stillness of a stretched bow vibrating with the energy of death, from the bow's limbs to the string, until the impassive arrow channels the power and turns an ordinary, useless object into a deadly instrument.

In our office, around us, there are agents who are bows, others who are string, and yet others who are arrows, resting right now, but who in two hours and forty-eight minutes will fill themselves with energy and be propelled onto targeted employees.

There is no reason, statistical or logical, that the battle that started at 08:00 will not continue at 11:15.

We are agents. And as agents, we finish our work.

We don't leave things dangling. We don't interrupt our task. We do everything we can to get the job done. At 11:15, the office will ignite again. The tiny possibility that what is certain will not come to pass puts this prediction in jeopardy, but after all, if nothing happens, and no one attacks anyone, Laszlo's plan will be easier to execute. In any case, this is the right strategy.

[chan#M256] LASZLO: I'll meet you at 11:15.

[chan#M256] LASZLO: I'm warning you: if the door to your cubicle isn't open,

[chan#M256] LASZLO: I'll force it open and kill you myself.

[chan#M256] THÉODORE: Okay, okay.

[chan#M256] THÉODORE: It'll be open.

It's the most sensible option.

Being with Théodore during the attack is the best guarantee that he won't mess it all up.

Hick will meet up with Solveig and help her as far as sector Z.

He's a good egg, Laszlo thinks.

The guild's private channel is silent.

And nothing is being posted on [chan#9926], because no one wants to raise the subject of Clara's death. But everyone is thinking about it, regretting the loss of such a brilliant surgeon and delighting that they were not named the guilty party in the Copiers' counter-investigation.

Except for Laszlo, who saw Clara slit her own throat before disappearing, we are shivering imagining the nightmare in which we believe she has just landed.

What is she doing right now? How is she handling the shame of no longer having a job? Is she lying on the ground at the foot of the towers? Is she waiting, half-dead, for a futile act, a pointless thought, every second of her life now burdened with the weight of dishonour? Or is she walking, aimlessly, without shelter, straight ahead, in the street, and will she continue to walk until she perishes from exhaustion?

Not talking about Clara spares us from picturing even more terrible hypotheses, never knowing which is the right one.

And we work, trying not to think about Clara, trying not to think about the street, and particularly trying not to think about the violence that will soon be unleashed.

We don't manage to concentrate enough to forget that at 11:10 the aisles will start to howl again and that, perhaps, one of us will be about to live their final hour.

The company will notice, and it will criticize the few minutes of flagging attention, but the comments will appear only tomorrow on the personalized news feed. If we read them, it will mean we are still alive, and this reality will be enough to bury the shame of having temporarily become less efficient at work.

[chan#W889] LASZLO: Be ready.
[chan#W889] LASZLO: You head out of your cubicle, and you meet up with Solveig.

[chan#W889] LASZLO: She'll tell you what to do next.
[chan#W889] HICK: Okay.


Laszlo stands up and watches the conversation disappear, wondering whether this is the last time he will type on a keyboard. If everything goes well, it is.

He grabs the steaming cup on his desk and takes a swig of coffee.

Then he walks slowly to the door of his cubicle.

It is 11:11. The break is in four minutes.

He opens the door soundlessly and heads out into the corridor holding his breath.

He stands in the middle of the empty aisle and waits.

In front of him, after the first intersection, sectors T and S are bathed in blue morning light that is starting to turn to the greyish-white light of midday.

Nothing is happening. No sound reaches him either.

The fires that were burning when he returned to his cubicle less than three hours ago have had time to go out on their own, smothered by the partly fireproof materials of the office.

But, mainly, nothing is happening.

The company makes no comment to him. No voice rings out ordering him back to his cubicle.

He is alone in the office corridors, outside of the fifteen-minute break.

He smiles and starts walking quickly toward sector K, which he reaches at 11:14.

Along the way, he tries to mentally calculate the exact number of seconds that have gone by.

He gets it right; twenty seconds remain before the break when he grabs the doorknob for Théodore's cubicle.

At that very moment, Hick turns up the collar of his purple tunic, imagining that the layer of fabric will protect his face from the more benign projectiles, and he too puts his hand on the doorknob.

Which enemy is doing likewise behind the partition? How many have already scaled the walls of their cubicle to take aim at him? How many will arrive as reinforcements in the first ten seconds of the attack?

Hick tells himself that, when it comes down to it, escape might not be such a bad solution. But then what?

Too late. There is no time to think about it, because already an explosion reverberates in the distance.

It's the break.

He grits his teeth and hurls himself out the door, under the self-propelled projectiles, the bullets, and the paralyzing darts fired in every direction.

Laszlo throws a smoke grenade in the corridor and goes into Théodore's cubicle, having doubted the door would be open.

Théodore jumps, eyes wide open at this temporal disconnect.

'But …,' he stammers. 'How did you get here so quickly?'

'I ran,' Laszlo answers simply. 'Take down the wire mesh; we need to be able to respond.'

'But we don't have any weapons,' Théodore wails.

Laszlo pulls two handguns from under his jacket and reveals a belt of grenades that produce different effects. He throws a gun, which Théodore catches, almost losing his balance.

'If you knew how hard it is for me to leave this in your hands, but I have no choice. Just try not to shoot at me.'

Théodore appears paralyzed by this new responsibility. He never would have thought that one day he would be holding a firearm.

Our guild is, and has always been, a defensive guild. We don't have weapons. Only our words, our intellect, our strategies, and the armour on our cubicles, into which we sink all our savings during the annual shopping window. It's a policy that has allowed us to survive so far.

'If anything comes through this door,' Laszlo says, 'you shoot. And if anything drops from above, you grab it fast and throw it even faster.'

He jumps over Théodore's desk, removes the screen and the keyboard, which he places on the floor, then pushes the desk against the partition wall.

In the office, the commotion and howling increase in intensity. The noise level of the explosions, gunshots, impacts, and cries makes it seem like the ground itself is shaking, as if the whole floor has just found its resonating frequency and is now at risk of imploding, a survival reflex of a building in danger.

Laszlo climbs onto Théodore's desk and empties his clip over the partition wall without looking where he is firing. He takes a box of bullets from his pocket and reloads his gun, as the response can already be heard, burning metal smashing into the cold metal of the armoured wall a few centimetres from Laszlo's head.

'Shit, shit,' Théodore says. 'What time is it?'

It's 11:17, and Hick is hurrying toward Solveig's cubicle.

The second Hick shouts his colleague's name, the door opens, and he charges inside without noticing that the corridor is relatively calm.

He collapses to the ground with a sigh of relief.

Then he turns onto his back and freezes when he sees Solveig.

She is buck naked, standing in front of him, her silhouette like a suit of hairless, taut white skin standing out against the black of the partition walls.

But it's not the nudity that stuns Hick or the fact that there is no hair growing on the flawless skin. It's the stomach. An enormous, bulging stomach. An impossible stomach, which he imagines is the result of an unknown illness Solveig has contracted. A stomach he thinks he sees moving at times, as if Solveig's guts have a life of their own and are knocking at the door of her body like the attackers on the door of her cubicle, to toy with her nerves, during the eight o'clock break.

'Your…,' he says, with difficulty. 'Your stomach…'

'Ah,' she says. 'Laszlo didn't tell you…'

She goes to her desk and opens a drawer without saying anything further.

There's not much time.

Explaining how she got pregnant, how the egg resulting from this pregnancy grew, how it made her vomit and deformed her, so that today her stomach is this grotesque and heavy sphere that weighs on her, telling of the day she realized she couldn't put on her jumpsuit anymore, or the day she felt the enormous thing she was carrying move inside her – explaining everything would take too much time. Which they don't have.

She pulls from the drawer a sheet of paper that she holds out to Hick. On it, black lines mark out the borders of sector Z and a red line shows the route to the Up and Down Door.

Hick looks at the sheet, incredulous.

'What's this?'

'It's the map,' Solveig says. 'So we don't get lost in sector Z.'

'Yes, but this,' Hick says, pointing to the sheet.

'Ah.' Solveig gets it. 'It's paper. You can write on it. We don't use it often, but we will today. You're going to have to lend me your tunic.'

Hick, understanding that the explanation of the paper will stop there, puts the sheet in his pocket.

He has no intention of dawdling. He removes his purple tunic. His lace shirt and his velvet pants are stained with brown splatters. He helps Solveig put on the tunic. Despite the ample fabric, she can't do up the buttons over her large stomach.

It's better than nothing, they think, before moving toward the door.

'Ready?' Hick asks.

Solveig responds with a concentrated nod of the head.

The next second, at 11:20, they are in the corridor, heads down, hunched, their bodies rushing forward.

The first corridor is still calm, and Solveig wonders why there are no battles being waged in her sector, when the rest of the office is erupting and burning. The two colleagues turn at the corner of sectors Q and P and head down the central aisle.

Unconsciously, they slow their pace in seeing the few dozen metres that separate them from sector Z, straight ahead.

The central aisle is unrecognizable. Furniture is placed crosswise along the passage as barricades for agents who must have been driven out of their cubicles by tear gas. At regular intervals, deadly projectiles shoot out of the corridors and get caught in partition walls across the way, ricochet when there is a lot of armouring, and even sometimes lodge in the bodies of agents, who scream upon contact with the metal, and collapse, hemorrhaging, begging to be finished off or continuing to fire blindly with what little is left of their lives.

'My leg, my leg,' screams a sprawled-out red-headed woman whose leg, from the middle of the shin on down, has flown into another sector, swept away on the blast of a violent explosion. 'I can't get back to my cubicle! Kill me! I don't want to end up on the street!'

A bullet grants her request immediately. Solveig and Hick quickly step around her still body.

Hick's tunic lifts behind Solveig, who has given up holding it down, preferring to keep her hands free for balance.

The green border of sector Z is not far away. Hick tries to make a path, doing his best to clear the objects, bodies, and debris slowing their progress. When a barricade seems too heavy, he leapfrogs onto the agent behind it and helps Solveig step over the obstacle.

At the entrance to sectors U and T, the battle is less vicious and the plumes of black smoke that obstruct their view are thinner.

Solveig and Hick can finally make out, right in front of them, the plant barrier that marks the entrance to sector Z. Seen from here, it seems impenetrable, but according to Laszlo's map, there is an access point some twenty metres to the east.

Hick slows his pace and signals to Solveig to move ahead of him. The coast is clear. They just have to hurry, and logically the one in front will enjoy the effect of surprise and will have a better chance of getting through these final metres unharmed.

But the calm in the aisle is an illusion.

As soon as she steps into the line of sight of agents hunkered down in their cubicles, Solveig hears bullets whistling past her ears.

Several times, she even feels the projectiles pierce the purple tunic that floats behind her.

Reaching the corridor along sector Z, she veers slightly to the right and seeks, in the huge climbing jungle that covers almost the entire north side of the tower, what could resemble a passage.

The plant wall has reached the ceiling, and climbing plants have wound themselves around air, water, and electricity ducts and the switching module. An informed agent, familiar with botanical nomenclature from the global network, would recognize in this tangle of stems, leaves, and flowers varieties such as ficus, yucca, birthwort, grevillea, and giant papyrus, but they would be perplexed by most of the plants, hybrids of hybrids, which over decades, perhaps centuries, have mutated from clearly defined varieties of indoor horticulture. Left to its own devices for long enough, but supplied with fluids and minerals by a hydroponic system that is still working, the tropical jungle has grown, unfettered, covering this part of the office, which the old maps indicate used to have cubicles and agents, like any other sector. Instead of this seemingly impenetrable forest, there were partitions, desks, and machines where the numbers of the modern world scrolled by. And while no one was certain, people said it was a major health incident that forced agents occupying these cubicles to temporarily leave their posts. Then the temporary became permanent, until nature took over the empty spaces and, from being pleasant decor, the plant organisms become the area's sole owners.

Solveig believes she has arrived at the place on the map and, while uncertain of what will result from her gesture, she stretches her hand toward a giant leaf, a distant cousin of the banana tree. She has time to feel on her palm the cool, dewy caress of the plant, then collapses on the earthy, mossy ground, in the humid dusk of sector Z.

She gets up and waits two seconds, then three, then four, but Hick is nowhere to be seen.

She approaches the wall of thick leaves and furtively raises a branch to study the area around it.

It is 11:24. The corridor that runs along the jungle is deserted. Muffled blasts reverberate in the main aisle, and others, more violent, can be heard here and there around the office, rumours of the twilight of this era.

Solveig doesn't take the time to think or calculate the odds and turns her back to the office to advance along the humus path.

After all, she thinks, Hick has the map. If he is still alive, he will be able to find the Up and Down Door. Or else he will go get Laszlo and follow him to the roof, assuming Laszlo is also alive.

And he is.

He is standing on Théodore's desk and firing in the direction of the slightest movement detected in the bathrooms across the corridor.

The break will be over in six minutes, and the assailants know that it is time to throw the last of what they have into battle. Spending a third break storming the same cubicle would be a deadly waste of time. They have to wrap it up right now, and, to signal this decision to the defenders, they unleash ten tear gas, smoke, and explosive grenades, which fly over the corridor, rebound, and roll into Théodore's cubicle.

Paralyzed by the sight of this, Théodore drops his gun. His terrified eyes move between the grenades and Laszlo, as if begging him to tell him what to do.

But Laszlo has long stopped giving instructions. He jumps off the desk, kicks it to overturn it, grabs Théodore by the jacket and throws him down on the ground beside him, behind the armoured work surface, sheltered from explosions.

The hiss of tear gas and smoke grenades that spread their irritating gas is covered up by three explosions that rock the inside of the cubicle. The blast drives back the protective desk, wedging Laszlo and Théodore between the partition wall and the metal of the crumpled furniture.

The smoke and gas plunge the cubicle into darkness, and, when he opens his eyes, Laszlo thinks he sees in front of him cryptic numbers. He then sees that these symbols are engraved on the underside of the mangled desk that has just saved his life. Beside him, Théodore smiles.

'It's my calendar,' he says, beaming. 'My calendar saved me again!'

Laszlo decides not to explain to Théodore that what he has taken for a mystical calendar all these years is nothing more than the long serial number for the desk, engraved under all the desks of all the agents in the world.

The tear gas takes effect, and soon the image of Théodore's idiot smile grows clouded and disappears behind a curtain of tears and smoke.

Théodore, also blinded, feels Laszlo's hands grip his and close them around what remains of his desk. He then hears the telltale sound of the door of his cubicle opening and Laszlo's voice rising above the din of gunfire and explosions.

'We can't stay here,' he says. 'We push the desk into the corridor, and we stay behind it all the way!'

Théodore thinks the plan makes sense and pushes the desk toward the door he believes is open. Even with his eyes rendered useless by the gas, he knows exactly where to go. It's his cubicle. No one knows it better than him, and he could even dance in it, eyes closed, without bumping into a piece of furniture.

As a result, getting the desk out into the aisle takes only a few seconds. As soon as he recognizes the texture of the carpet in the corridor, a much shorter pile than the one in his cubicle, he orients the desktop to face the bathrooms and lies down behind it, jumping every time a projectile lands.

It is 11:26. Solveig arrives at the point Laszlo indicated the night before, when he drew her the map.

The waning light tells her that she has reached the end of the sector. The north wall must be behind this plant barrier. Beyond that, there are towers, covering the south quarter, further on the coral quarter, and further still the magnificent white towers of the nacre quarter, where Cily Vinière lives. Solveig imagines that, opposite her, tens of kilometres away, the heiress is putting on one of her luxurious travel outfits and looking in Solveig's direction. She doesn't know it, but they have a rendezvous, she thinks.

Solveig reaches another wall of branches and leaves, which she parts, the vegetation not putting up any real resistance. Tendrils of creepers and climbing plants have been torn off, no doubt by Laszlo, and Solveig concludes that she is at the right place.

She lifts a heavy palm leaf that hides a tall, shiny door, set in a concrete column that rises to the ceiling, which the plants have climbed to get their leaves closer to the artificial fluorescent lights. On the right side of the door, there is a rudimentary control panel, similar to the vending machines, although with far fewer options.

From this spot in sector Z, the din of the battle being waged in the office is a mere rumble, and only the lowest frequencies and vibrations from the floor reach Solveig, who finally feels safe.

She presses the only button on the panel that is not locked.

Emitting a quiet, high-pitched sound, the shiny door opens with two sliding panels that reveal a cabin about three metres square, gleaming, decorated with mirrors and gold gilding.

Roof, Solveig thinks.

It's the enigmatic name of the button Laszlo told her to press once she had gone through the Up and Down Door.

She takes a step forward, and her right foot, soiled with dirt, encounters the metal floor of the cabin. She shivers, as much because of the change of temperature that grips her as from the fear that she is living her final moments.

She puts her left foot in the cabin and sighs.

There.

She has left the office. At that very second, she is no longer an agent. And yet she is not dead, or fired, or in freefall from the top of a tower. She is just free.

Entirely incomprehensibly, she feels such relief at this idea that she starts to smile and even bursts out laughing with satisfaction.

A huge weight has just lifted. A weight she was carrying for so long that she wasn't even aware it was pressing down on and constraining her. In comparison, the heavy thing lodged in her uterus suddenly seems light, and she would even go so far as to say it is pleasant to have it as a companion. A burden a moment ago, a companion now, on which she places her hands to feel it moving, imagining that it approves of what she is doing.

She quickly finds the interior control panel Laszlo told her about.

A touch screen, built into the car, offers exactly 301 choices.

To the left of each button, a number is indicated, from 1 to 300, and to the left of the button 301 shine the letters 'Roof.'

Solveig is calm.

She doesn't think about what is going to happen to her in the next few minutes or what she will say to Cily Vinière-Banks to convince her to save her. She feels soothed, whole, simply because she is free, released from work to just be a woman, herself, without having to account to a guild or a machine. Just her, in a place that is already no longer the office.

She laughs, a boisterous, genuine laugh. A laugh that surprises her for its power, because she has never unleashed such joy. A laugh that resonates so loudly in the confined space that it prevents her from hearing the frantic steps approaching along the humus path.

She can only jump and emit a small cry when a human form jumps into the cabin and collapses on the control panel, lighting up some one hundred buttons, including the roof button, which immediately triggers the closing of the sliding doors of the Up and Down Door, the time-worn mechanics of which can be heard.

It is a little past 11:28, and Théodore starts to get his vision back after much drying of tears on the sleeve of his jacket.

He is crouched behind the desk, on the corridor carpet, deafened by the sound of the impact on his makeshift shield.

He lifts his head slightly, looking for Laszlo, who he thought had been at his side during the two endless minutes, but he doesn't see him. He is left to his own devices, unarmed, in the middle of the aisle, at the mercy of a bullet that could pierce the metal of his already seriously damaged desktop, or of a possible grenade.

'Laszlo,' he cries. 'Where the hell are you?'

The only response is more intense gunfire from the bathroom.

Maybe Laszlo didn't hear him call out, his voice covered up by the deafening noise of combat. Or did he answer, but Théodore couldn't hear his response because of the commotion?

He cries out again, as loud and long as he can.

Still nothing.

'You're all alone,' cries a voice a few metres from him. 'That'll teach you to play the smartass with the SB!'

Théodore realizes that Laszlo is no longer there, or that he is dead: if the Brigadier in the room across the way heard his call, Laszlo would have heard it too. For the two remaining minutes before work resumes, he has to make the decisions himself.

But how? Of all the tasks that an agent has to do, making decisions is the one Théodore never wanted to accept. He used to consult his calendar, and during the months that followed the last date entered, the guild had decided the little he had to accomplish.

Disoriented, Théodore studies the numbers entered under his desk. Maybe he forgot a detail?

Maybe a last date is ordering him to take a final action that will miraculously extract him from this final situation?

But still, nothing.

He knows the dates he is reading. All of them. He did what they were ordering him to do to the letter. But the calendar has run dry. It has fallen silent. As have Laszlo and the other members of the guild who could have come to his rescue. Théodore is powerless, paralyzed by the sudden responsibility that is forcing him to take care of himself.

When an explosive grenade ricochets off the outside of his cubicle and rolls to his feet, he doesn't even think about sending it back where it came from.

He jumps to his disabled feet and locks his eyes on the floor-to-ceiling window at the end of the corridor. In the second that he stands up, without protection against the heavy fire coming from across the way, he is hit with a half-dozen projectiles that he scarcely feels pierce his flesh.

His peculiar balance tilts him forward and starts him off running, not really bothered by the bullets that riddle him as he advances down the corridor, in constant acceleration, like a child who barely knows how to walk learning to run to make up for his lost balance.

Théodore runs straight ahead, and he doesn't know whether the tears streaming down his cheeks are due to the residue of the tear gas or to sadness and fear at the burning realization that this is his last run.

Cubicle walls stream by on either side of him, and he doesn't care about projectiles emerging from them, because he is already riddled with bullets, already dead, a cadaver galloping along the launch pad of his final voyage.

The cabin of the elevator in sector Z starts moving at 11:29, at the exact moment Théodore goes through – without feeling anything – the east window on the 122nd floor, which Solveig and a gravely injured Hick are leaving at an average speed of six metres per second.

A screen lights up above the sliding doors of the cabin and indicates a number, 122, quickly replaced by 123 and so on up to 126, at the appearance of which the elevator slows to a stop at the 127th floor, the first that Hick unwittingly requested when he collapsed on the control panel.

Solveig bends over to examine the injuries sustained by Hick, who is bleeding heavily, as the elevator doors open on the 127th floor.

The vision of chaos offered by the 127th floor is the same as on the 118th floor, in front of which Théodore passes furtively in his long fall to the street. It is a vision of battles and random killing, where everyone is attacking everyone else, where despite the imminent return to work, agents are not considering going back to their posts but are continuing the territorial fight started that morning.

The doors close again, and the cabin starts moving and stops, a few floors higher, on the same horror show, while Théodore, whipped by the winds of his own ingress into the air, makes out through each window he passes identical tableaus, like artistic compositions: mangled desks, lacerated agents, explosions with motionless flames, a maelstrom of violence that doesn't seem to have spared the lower floors either.

Solveig, Hick, and Théodore understand that the fury unleashed this morning was only partially related to the incident in the cafeteria or the introduction of the Solidarity Loan. Fury was brewing on every floor in the tower, maybe in every tower in the modern world. The smell of attack had spread and contaminated all humans, pitching them against one another in a battle to the death. The entire tower had become a battlefield from which only the bravest among us would get through. The others would be torn apart, broken, then deleted from the list of agents.

It takes less time for Théodore to reach the ground than for Solveig and Hick to reach the top of the tower, and the elevator stops at the 182nd floor as Théodore disappears into the thick fog that cloaks the base of the Chicago 3 towers. Since there is nothing more to see or to understand, he closes his eyes and enjoys the fresh air rushing into his nostrils for a few seconds more.

The sliding doors open on the 182nd floor, plunged in a thick black smoke that fills the car. Before the doors close again, Solveig and Hick hear someone call out to them, pleading and choking, a few metres away.

'Laszlo,' the voice asks, 'is that you? It's not too – '

A gunshot silences the agent, and the doors slide closed again. The elevator takes with it Solveig and Hick, who are wondering if they really just heard what they just heard.

As they go up, Solveig tears off Hick's embroidered shirt, the white of which has been stained scarlet at its centre. She wipes the blood with what remains of the fabric and examines the wound, which she quickly identifies as being due to a bullet from a small-calibre weapon. On the other side, there is another hole in the skin on Hick's back, and she concludes that the bullet went straight through.

If Hick isn't dead, it's because his organs weren't hit, and he has a chance of making it. She fashions a makeshift bandage with the shirt, which she cinches around her colleague's torso.

The trip up lasts a little over five minutes, every opening of the doors confirming to the two occupants of the elevator that all floors of the tower have succumbed to the same murderous madness.

These successive visions over more than thirty floors, all identical, set up with the same cubicles, populated by the same agents, in normal times busy on the same screens, illuminated by the same machines, comfort Solveig in her resolve to leave this nightmarish world, without life or beauty, as quickly as possible, a world dedicated to work and forgetting who we are and, more than anything, who we could be.

Finally, at 11:35, the cabin of the Up and Down Door stops at the top floor of tower 35S, the floor labelled Roof on the control panel. For the first time, a cool, gentle wind blows into the car, accompanied by the unfathomable light of a cloudy sky, although much less overcast than normal.

Solveig and Hick squint so as not to be blinded, and the mother-to-be helps her colleague stand and then take the few steps that separate them from freedom and Cily Vinière-Banks's aircraft, which should be here soon.

They are barely out of the elevator before the doors close; the control panel warns that the cabin is going to go back down, without Solveig or Hick noticing it, both stunned by the panorama before them.

They advance slowly along a rough concrete surface, blackened by rain and partially covered with dark green moss a centimetre or two high. The surface of the roof, as one would imagine, is equal to the surface of the 122nd floor, but even Solveig, occupant of the office for much longer than Hick, did not realize how vast the space was. Cloistered since the beginning of our lives in tiny cubicles, in turn circumscribed in sectors, fractions of surfaces, we have never had call to imagine how big the area of our floor would be if it were rid of its cubicles, the constraining partition walls, and the requisite furniture.

The block of smooth concrete two metres high that houses the Up and Down Door is the only visible protrusion to disrupt the flat expanse of the roof, and Solveig, with her pathological desire for perfection, is surprised to want this monstrosity to disappear too, leaving intact the fabulous platform on which she keeps advancing with Hick at her side.

She loosens her grip. Even though he seems in a strange state, which she attributes to the amount of blood he has just lost, her colleague can walk without assistance.

'I don't even know, Solveig,' he says weakly. 'What time is it? I can't miss the end of the break.'

'You have time,' she lies. 'We have time.'

Reassured, Hick stops and lets his eyes wander to the thick layer of clouds crawling by above their heads.

Solveig steps around the Up and Down Door and heads toward the edge of the roof. It is encircled by a parapet a half metre high, probably to prevent people from tipping over accidentally.

Solveig takes a few more steps and can make out, on the other side of the parapet, beyond a three-hundred-metre gap, the deserted roof of another tower of equal height, which appears to be next to another roof, the summit of another tower, and another one, and so on until the horizon, but also to the right, to the left, behind, a concrete carpet extending in every direction, a massive grid at the top of the modern world, where buildings, unsurprisingly, are identical in height, the spaces between the buildings equal, and their surface area the same.

Before this ground above the ground, this infinite expanse of flat, geometric concrete, Solveig forgets that she is walking at hundreds of metres of altitude, and that below, far below, in the intervals of emptiness, at level zero of the universe, there is the street, an invisible black space, perpetually bathed in dense fog and the shadow of the towers.

'What's good about here,' yells Hick, who seems to have recovered his strength, 'is that it's the only place where you will never see a body fall by a window. It's peaceful.'

Solveig turns, smiling, to answer him, and the muscles of her body contract as she sees a dark shape charge at her.

A few minutes earlier, a molecule of caffeine fell into an esophagus deprived of light and found itself, eight seconds later, in a murky stomach, where digestive juices started to attack it, then, still intact, resolute against the assaults of the enzymes and acids, reached the duodenum, where it continued its route to try to infiltrate, a bit further on, the walls of the small intestine, which it passed through easily. Mixed in with the blood, it made its short journey as far as the brain, completely unaware of the fact that around it, behind the dark red barrier of flesh and skin, an even more terrible war was being waged. Near receptors normally devoted to the molecule adenosine, it stopped its course and attached itself to them, reversing the orders sent to the heart and to the glands secreting adrenaline to significantly increase blood pressure and heart rate. This surplus of energy, combined with other even more complex factors, activates the muscles of Laszlo's legs, torso, and arms, to allow him to push Solveig with all his might.

This energy, propelled horizontally by Laszlo's movement, is transferred into the body of Solveig, who, in turn, picks up speed and travels the few metres that separate her from the concrete para-pet she collides with. That is when the energy that fills Solveig, finding an obstacle along its route, triggers two fundamental forces of this world: gravity and centrifugal force.

First, the kinetic energy instigated by Laszlo presses on Solveig's shoulders to tip her over and spin her on an axis that meets with the ridge of the parapet. Then, once in rotation, the powerless body reverses under the effect of centrifugal force, Solveig's feet lift from the ground, and her pelvis travels some ten centimetres further, into the void.

Then gravity lays claim to this physical object, subject like all others to earthly attraction, and propels it toward the ground at an initial speed of 0.2 metres per second, which then increases to the rate of 9.81 metres per second squared, until it encounters one last obstacle: the street.

Hick, who has just witnessed the scene, is not thinking about these laws of physics. He remains prostrate, with – printed in the periphery of his field of vision – the image of Solveig, just before she disappears into the void without the slightest cry, not even of surprise. Despite the scientific certainty that human persistence of vision is only fifty milliseconds, he thinks he can still see before him, on the other side of the concrete parapet, the naked silhouette wrapped in his purple tunic.

Laszlo turns toward him, looking sombre, and puts his hand in his pocket.

Hick realizes he is going to die. This time, it's certain. Laszlo is going to take out a weapon and kill him.

He doesn't know what to say to him. He is in pain. A thought comes to him: he has not been an agent for long, but he has been an original agent, dressed originally and acting originally, and dying the same way, killed by a member of his own guild on the roof of his tower, like no other agent before him.

He doesn't close his eyes and utters a single sentence before Laszlo carries out his act.

'So, you're the one who set all this off?'

Laszlo takes his recorder out of his pocket. He doesn't smile, despite the satisfaction that fills him in this precise moment of the end of the story of the modern world.

'I explain everything on there,' he says. 'And if you have time, you can take a look at my films and photos on the public network too. Everything is online. Good luck, Hick.'

He tosses the recorder at Hick, who catches it with difficulty and a grimace of pain.

Then, without waiting for a reaction, or a response, or advice, and without the slightest hesitation either, Laszlo straddles the parapet and throws himself into the void, at exactly 11:41.

Hick is alone on the roof, bare-chested, wounded, wrapped in a bandage, Laszlo's recorder in his hand, and nowhere, not in any direction, is there a personnel representative; no flying vehicle of one hypothetical Cily Vinière-Banks is in sight.

He doesn't wait a moment longer and with difficulty heads to the Up and Down Door. He presses the play button on the recorder.

'There is no such thing as the end of the world,' Laszlo's voice says. 'What we call the end of the world is a cat running and turning the corner of a corridor…'

Hick summons the elevator by hitting the control panel, but he doesn't need to wait. The elevator is already there. It carried Laszlo here, and there is no reason for anyone on a lower floor to have used it since. The sliding doors slide. Hick steps into the cabin and presses the 122nd floor. As the doors close, he does it again with all the other buttons, from the 300th to the 123rd.

So the elevator stops at every floor, for a few seconds, and each time the doors reveal an apocalyptic landscape: ravaged desks, broken cubicles, smoking carpets, bodies being sprayed with acid clouds. It is this real-life film, this painting of blood and ashes, that the ghost of Laszlo narrates the whole way down, explaining blow by blow the complex plan that led to this Armageddon.

'It all started with cubicle 314,' the voice says. 'If I hadn't discovered Élisabeth, we would still be behind our screens, hard at work, stultified by the repetition of tasks, afraid of the eventuality of doing them wrong. But I found her. I saw her with my own eyes. In cubicle 314 of sector Y1. And it changed everything.'

At the 282nd floor, carbon clouds put out the last of a fire that has ravaged the entire office. The smell is so unbearable that Hick is overcome with a coughing fit that intensifies the pain of his wound. The doors finally close, and the cabin resumes its journey.

'For months,' Laszlo's voice continues, 'I examined Élisabeth's skeleton, intact, which no acid cloud had started into or even come near. It was insects that cleaned her, bacteria that relieved her of her blackened flesh. What did she die of? I don't know. But I know she died in silence and that the smell of her body hadn't bothered any of her neighbours. Forgotten by the agents. Forgotten by the company. Luckily, I found her, I was there for her, to remember that, in the distant past, she worked, she suffered, she gave her life for a company that didn't care about her. And I thought: who does the company really care about? If an agent can die unnoticed, does the company really need us? That's where my great work was born. It was from that egg of disgust that it hatched and grew. Whoever is listening, I want you to realize how alone we were, and idiotic, and pathetic, and miserable. I want you to realize how much what I did has lifted us up – not just me, but all of us.'

Two hundred and sixty-fifth floor: silence. Hick sticks his head out the open doors and looks around. The cubicles are intact, the carpet blue, the aisles clean. If a cubicle could be forgotten, could an entire floor be as well, all its agents dead and never replaced? Hick wants to step out, open the door of a cubicle to check whether inside there is a screen disseminating information personalized for a skeleton, and the same thing in all the other cubicles. But he decides against it. It could also be a trap, or a new weapon, or a malfunction of the flow-switching module that wiped out the agents by having them breathe their own excrement. It is wiser to leave. The doors close.

Hick leans on the wall of the cabin and lets himself slide to the floor. His abdomen hurts. He listens to the rest of the message with his eyes closed while the ravaged floors go by.

'I would have liked to have spared Clara,' Laszlo says. 'But there was no logical reason to do so. Only passionate reasons, the sort of reason that has no place in great works. So, I filmed her during her operation, and I sent the video to the Copiers. I think she was smart enough to understand that I was the one responsible for her undoing.

'I saw it in her eyes, when she went through the 8-Char Door and slit her throat without looking at me, looking only at the camera that she knew was responsible for her death.'

The voice on the recorder pauses. The sliding doors open onto new carnage, then close again. The cabin resumes its descent.

'Théodore was simple. I just had to photograph him after his operation and send his description to the Brigadiers. After that, it was obvious the attack would be launched that very morning. I have no regrets about him. Théodore wasn't cut out for our guild. I'm not even sure he was cut out for this world. As for Solveig, I had to handle that personally, because our fates were tied. Now they will be forever.'

Hick is having a hard time thinking. And a hard time deciding whether what he is hearing is the fruit of admirable perfection or abominable cruelty.

'Thermodynamics is not a science,' Laszlo continues. 'It's an art. An art I learned to control, since the day the scope of my awareness was no longer limited to the tiny frontiers of our office. When I discovered the Up and Down Door, my field of vision expanded, possibility was revealed, and I understood that the battles waged, the cubicles taken from other guilds, all the action that we can take in the closed framework of the office is just the obligatory result of a larger design. What we take for decisions were only movements comparable to the wiggle of particles subjected to forces that are greater than them. Even I was just an infinitesimal pawn in the global gears. The thought of it was unbearable. So I studied. I joined the discussion channels for the tower, the closed networks, and the private dialogue boxes of the guilds. I took notes. I evaluated the system, not limiting myself to the balance of power on just our floor, but picturing tower 35S as a physical structure I had to throw off course. My computer took years to calculate the likelihood of the success of my work, to accurately identify the key points of the system that when disrupted would cause a general collapse. Years of waiting during which I survived only to savour the satisfaction of this day. My only regret is not having a higher-performance machine or a longer life, because these constants would have allowed me to apply my plan to the entire city, or even more widely. For months now, since the results of the thermodynamic analysis were presented to me, I've taken advantage of every moment to attack the nerve centres of the system. I talk with other guilds, on other floors, maybe ten, tops, but those who are unwittingly the keystones of the tower, those who are, because of their location or their particular qualities, the most powerful forces of equilibrium in this building and whose undoing would threaten the entire structure. I followed to the letter the plan that my machine developed. I met in person with agents whose fate was crucial. I set the scene; I had the actors rehearse. All that remained for me this morning was to raise the curtain. If someone is listening to these recorded words right now, it is because I achieved my goal. I managed to become someone in a world where no one is anything.'

Hick stops the recording. The doors open on the 182nd floor, where Solveig and Hick thought they heard Laszlo's name spoken by a silhouette engulfed in smoke. What they had interpreted as a hallucination or a coincidence a few minutes earlier now appeared to be reality. That voice, thinks Hick, must have been one of the key agents Laszlo met to foment his deadly plan, passing for an employee on the same floor, for a Veep, or for someone else.

The elevator doors close, and Hick goes back to listening to the audio file.

'So, why?' Laszlo says. 'That must be what you're asking, whoever is listening to me. Why do it? Accomplish what I accomplished? Yes, there is the beauty of the act. This beauty that we tried to get closer to all these years. But is it truly beautiful? And beautiful for whom, if the very creator of this masterpiece cannot admire it? No. There is another reason, necessary and inevitable: to put an end to it. To put an end once and for all to the lie of our lives and the lie of our work. To the lie of ourselves, we who have never been anything. Without identity, without passion, without life, we were neutral and insignificant particles of a physical whole that could have continued perfectly well without us. We invented for ourselves peculiarities, tastes, but nothing that would distinguish us from those in the cubicle next door. Théodore cut off his toes, and Clara tormented her body, while Solveig shaved and plucked. And then what? Did it make us any different from each other? Did it make us unique? We think alike, we live alike. We all get up at the same time to do the same pointless tasks and take our daily routes down these decomposing aisles. There was nothing in our lives that could give us the will to look at tomorrow with more compassion than today. Today was as dead as tomorrow and yesterday, and as all the other days that we will spend waiting to be thrown out or die. Because that was the only thing we wanted. That was the only thing that would have truly transformed us: being thrown out or dying. We fought, and we tried to convince ourselves that these pathetic battles were important or useful, and that that's why we are here. But deep down, we all know that these battles had a single goal: to accidentally kill us. Being victorious once again meant facing the horror of being required to live another day, or another week, until the next battle that, unfortunately, might not kill us either. My work was to free the agents, to give them what they have long been looking for, much more than power or material possessions. Death – the relief of finally being dead. That is my work. That is what I accomplished. It is my work, and it is beautiful, because it is ephemeral. Soon, an army of replacements will walk through the 8-Char Doors on all floors in this tower. The cubicles will be rebuilt, the machines replaced, and work will resume like before. But you who are listening to me, you will know the truth. You will have experienced what we experienced and seen what we have seen. You will have visited cubicle 314 of sector Y1 on the 122nd floor, and you will have witnessed this end. Our end.'

Our end.

The end of us.

We who were a group, brothers and sisters, a guild.

We who are no longer anything.

That's what Laszlo wanted to say and what he has accomplished – the end of us.

So that the word will have lost its meaning.

We are no longer anything.

*We* is no longer anything. After this event, no one can say *we* because *we* will no longer mean anything. How do you say *we*, how do we be *we*, when even our closest colleagues betray us and kill us with no remorse? How do we continue to think that *we* has the slightest meaning, that we have the slightest meaning, when the only reason to be here is to kill as quickly as possible whoever is precisely not part of *we*. How do we continue to say *we* when we are unable to grasp all its power, and when this *we* has always been just a crude mask that hides an *I*?

We don't exist.

We have never existed. Since the beginning, the *we* that describes this world is nothing and no one. Not a guild, not an agent. We are no one. In this world, created as it was created, organized by its underlying perfection, kept alive by work that is our only horizon, *we* is no one, because it can't not be.

'So, you who are listening to me,' Laszlo's voice continues, 'you who are the last survivor of this tower purified by my masterpiece, you who knows how the world works, this world where there is no Cily Vinière, no Milton Banks, nothing but machines that pitch us from birth to death in front of other machines programmed to tell us the imaginary stories of a synthetic world. You who has understood that we are the ones who erected this world around our own fear, the fear of not having work, the fear of the street and of cats, who when you come down to it are just other living beings, maybe happy, maybe frolicking on the ground, laughing between the towers about the profound stupidity that has locked us away. You who are listening to me and who knows that what I am saying is true, I ask you this final question: do you finally know who you are?'

The doors slide open to reveal the thick jungle of sector Z of the 122nd floor.

Hick is back.

He presses the stop button on the recorder, gets back up clenching his teeth, exits the car, and then starts down the humus path.

It is 11:50 when he crosses the threshold and reaches the smoking remains of his workplace. Cubicles, although armoured, are partially melted, doors are riddled with holes where the little metal that remains is held only by minuscule junctions that you could break by blowing on them. Black smoke billows toward the ceiling, sucked up by the ventilation system. Fires are still burning in entire sectors, and there are not enough carbon clouds to control them all. The bodies of fallen agents who have not yet been reduced to dust by the cleaning clouds give off the appalling odour of roast pork, no shallots.

Bodies. Bodies in every square metre, bodies Hick avoids as he heads along the tortured aisles, some of which have disappeared, vast expanses previously bordered by cubicles that the violence of the battle has reduced to nothingness.

He approaches the west window at 11:53 and, despite his precautions and a careful search, he finds no trace of a living Brigadier. The corridor leading to his cubicle is littered with bodies and debris, provenance unknown.

He pushes open the door to his personal space. He feels like he left it centuries ago. A quick calculation confirms, however, that it was less than forty minutes ago.

He picks up his screen, his keyboard, sets them back on his desk, which he straightens, and sits on his slightly wobbly chair.

He turns his machine back on. His screen flickers.

Hick observes it with attention, sees the feeds fire up, sees that companies are created and others disappear, that Veeps live and die, that sports scores are piling up and with them the statistics for each match, that capital is expanding or contracting, that the modern world is turning, still here, ever infallible, that the massacre of tower 35S has not had the slightest impact on the general movement of the city, and even less of the world, a drop of water, dust, an insignificant $x$ in an equation with $x^{1000}$ unknowns, that agents disappear and others appear, motivated, proud, and joyful, prouder and more joyful still to have work that others don't have.

Seeing around him the crumbling partition walls riddled with bullets, thinking about the countless bodies piled in the destroyed aisles and the corridors of the office and of those that are lying in other offices in the tower, seeing the consequences of the horrible internecine massacre that killed all the agents in tower 35S except him, Hick has new hope and mentally calculates the number of hours left before hundreds of replacements stream through the 8-Char Door, replacements the institute has trained and who are ready to join the office, motivated, excited, enthusiastic, like he was a few months earlier, and also calculates the number of replacements he could kill during his fifteen-minute breaks, not all of them, unfortunately, but many, before the office reaches its initial head count and resumes operations like before.

Hick also thinks of his predecessors, with respect, of Solveig, Clara, Théodore, and mainly of Laszlo, who through his immoral action at least allowed Hick to put the odds of professional success on his side, all the advantage, all the cards in his mid-month replacement's hands on whom no Bookie would have wagered, all the chances to become the absolute master of the office, the uncontested head of the guild of guilds he imagines himself founding.

Hick smiles, then presses the play button on the recorder, to listen to Laszlo's final words again, to the essential and inevitable question that every agent, every day, should never stop asking.

'Do you finally know who you are?'

Surprised that he needed to think, even for a few seconds, about this question, addressing Laszlo on the other side, Hick answers with as much conviction he can muster, with an authoritative voice, which imposes respect down to the crackling of the cadavers whose burning is near an end:

'I am Agent Hick. I am in a good mood, and I will now get to work.'

**Grégoire Courtois** lives and works in Burgundy, where he runs the independent bookstore Obliques, which he bought in 2011. A novelist and playwright, he has published four novels with Le Quartanier: *Révolution* (2011), *Suréquipée* (2015), *Les lois du ciel* (2016), and *Les agents* (2019). *Les lois du ciel* was published by Coach House Books as *The Laws of the Skies* in 2019.

**Rhonda Mullins** is a writer and translator. She received the 2015 Governor General's Literary Award for *Twenty-One Cardinals*, her translation of Jocelyne Saucier's *Les héritiers de la mine. And the Birds Rained Down*, her translation of Jocelyne Saucier's *Il pleuvait des oiseaux*, was a CBC Canada Reads Selection. It was also shortlisted for the Governor General's Literary Award, as were her translations of Élise Turcotte's *Guyana* and Hervé Fischer's *The Decline of the Hollywood Empire*. She translated Grégoire Courtois's previous novel for Coach House Books. Rhonda currently lives in Montréal.

Typeset in Acier BAT, Slate Pro, and Arno.

Printed at the Coach House on bpNichol Lane in Toronto, Ontario, on Zephyr
Antique Laid paper, which was manufactured, acid-free, in Saint-Jérôme,
Quebec, from second-growth forests. This book was printed with vegetable-
based ink on a 1973 Heidelberg KORD offset litho press. Its pages were folded
on a Baumfolder, gathered by hand, bound on a Sulby Auto-Minabinda, and
trimmed on a Polar single-knife cutter.

Coach House is on the traditional territory of many nations, including the
Mississaugas of the Credit, the Anishnabeg, the Chippewa, the Haudenosau-
nee, and the Wendat peoples, and is now home to many diverse First Nations,
Inuit, and Métis peoples. We acknowledge that Toronto is covered by Treaty
13 with the Mississaugas of the Credit. We are grateful to live and work on
this land.

Edited by Alana Wilcox
Cover design by Ingrid Paulson
Interior design by Crystal Sikma
Author photo by Pascal Arnac-Pautrel, © Le Quartanier
Translator photo by Owen Egan

Coach House Books
80 bpNichol Lane
Toronto ON M5S 3J4
Canada

416 979 2217
800 367 6360

mail@chbooks.com
www.chbooks.com